VAIN SHADOW

Persephone Book Nº 112
Published by Persephone Books Ltd 2015

First published by Victor Gollancz and by
Charles Scribner's Sons, New York in 1963

Endpapers taken from a 1950s Heal's curtain material
which was used until the 1960s – provenance unknown,
in a private collection.

Typeset in ITC Baskerville by
Keystroke, Wolverhampton

Printed and bound in Germany by
GGP Media GmbH, Poessneck

9781910263020

Persephone Books Ltd
59 Lamb's Conduit Street
London WC1N 3NB
020 7242 9292

www.persephonebooks.co.uk

VAIN SHADOW

by

JANE HERVEY

with a new preface by

CELIA ROBERTSON

25/7/2015

London

PERSEPHONE BOOKS
LONDON

PREFACE

Vain Shadow, the portrait of a family funeral and its repercussions, is Jane Hervey's only published novel. She wrote it in the early 1950s, put it away in a drawer for nearly ten years, and it was eventually published in 1963.

By that time, women writers had begun to express themselves with more freedom and confidence than ever before. So it was that *Vain Shadow* came out in the same year as Sylvia Plath's *The Bell Jar*. *The Pumpkin Eater* by Penelope Mortimer and *The L-Shaped Room* by Lynne Reid Banks had been published just a year or so earlier. And, as Larkin's 'Annus Mirabilis' reminds us, the *Lady Chatterley* trial had been and gone, the pill was now available, and 1963 saw the release of The Beatles' first album.

In this context, *Vain Shadow* might have seemed a little old fashioned, but as a needle on the historical compass of the previous decade, it quivers with the anticipation of change, poised at the very end of what had gone before.

Despite the conventional setting, one soon realises that Jane Hervey's take on a death in the family is unique, astute and very funny. When she first submitted the novel to a

publisher they complained that they couldn't imagine why anyone would want to read about a funeral. But that is precisely this book's appeal; people behave strangely and badly around death and a family funeral has a dark comic drama all of its own.

The plot is simple; a wealthy family gathers at the family home (a 2,000 acre country estate in Derbyshire) in the aftermath of the patriarch's death; to mourn him, bury him and read his will. Jane Hervey restricts herself to four chapters, corresponding to four days, and the weight of the novel lies in the relationships between the old man's surviving wife and adult children as they begin to realise what his death will mean.

Full of dark inherited furniture, its windows dressed with swags of heavy fabric, tables laid with cut glass, Otterley Hall feels like the setting for an Agatha Christie novel. Most of the action takes place in the drawing room, the bedrooms and carpeted corridors of the house, the atmosphere thick with an apparently permanent conservatism. The present is in thrall to the past and seems to have no urgency of its own. But, as the four days unfold, the author reveals that things are on the point of changing forever.

We hardly leave the domestic setting – not even to walk in the garden. There are a couple of brief expeditions to the farm and the shops and there is the funeral itself, but otherwise we are stuck with the family – and they with each other. To the contemporary reader this gives the novel a televisual quality – as if we're following these people around with a camera, tracking them from room to room, looking

over the banisters to the hall below, sitting with them on the edge of a satin eiderdown. Every gesture, change of clothes, meal and argument is minutely detailed. One might baulk at the density of description and the lack of pace but the claustrophobia is deliberate. Relinquishing the desire to race, one is submerged in this family of thwarted ambitions and sibling rivalries and able to see what each character is looking for.

The focus is so intense that even their thoughts are overheard. From the first page, the surprising use of internal asides for each character means that the dialogue is constantly undercut by what each is really feeling – they are tripped up by unsolicited, shameful memories, caught out by their own trivial mental pictures and reactions. For this is a book about people who are unable to show or share their feelings, who are stumbling through the rituals and required etiquette demanded by the situation whilst not actually feeling any grief at all.

The dead man was a tyrant who belittled and stifled his wife and dominated his children to the point where they have all been damaged or sought escape. They have an idea of what is the right thing to do but are caught in the confusion of not feeling what they ought. How does one behave after the death of someone one should have loved and didn't? Banal thoughts filter into their heads, petty rivalry overrides anything more profound. So the relieved widow wonders if she'll now be able to have her much longed-for peach bathroom, her sons compete over logistical details and the only person to shed real tears is one of the servants.

Jane Hervey is brilliant on the power play within a family: who gets what and who does what in the vacuum left by a dead parent. She observes the struggle between husband and wife, child and parent, older and younger siblings, those with status and those without and how that status is achieved. Her novel is restless with these constantly shifting positions as the characters jostle and bicker for advantage. It is clear from early on how well the title (taken from 'The Burial of the Dead' in *The Book of Common Prayer*) fits this drama:

For man walketh in a vain shadow, and disquieteth himself in vain;
He heapeth up riches, and cannot tell who shall gather them.

Certain set pieces stick in the mind – the hilarious break-neck car journey to the cremation, the perfectly-judged division of treasures from a glass cabinet, so cleverly paced that the reader experiences everyone's anxiety and barely suppressed greed for each object.

Class differences are laid bare too. Jane Hervey's personal experience of living with domestic and estate servants makes the exchanges between the two sides vivid and plausible. The housekeeper Upjohn provides her perspective and the family's casual snobberies and assumptions are fully exposed. It is interesting that the servants seem to have a clearer idea of what to do in this crisis than the family they work for. Sobering also to realise that the master's death marks the end of the old ways. With the break up of the estate, they will lose their livelihoods and some will lose their homes.

These serious themes remain in the background while the immediate action often verges on farce. There is a freedom in Jane Hervey's observational humour which delights in the bathos of family exchanges. At one point the conversation, 'had passed from soup to zombies', at another the soufflé is described as 'light as a fart'.

Only a sister could observe her middle-aged brothers so finely – vying over which newspaper to take into the lavatory, arguing over how to eat a boiled egg, picking their noses, scratching their heads. The details accumulate to create an atmosphere of extreme male irritation and intense female anxiety.

On reading *Vain Shadow* for the first time, I did not realise how autobiographical it was, but when I met Jane Hervey in October 2013 she happily admitted to using her own family as a direct template. So easy was it for her siblings to spot this on publication (despite changes of names) that they found it deeply offensive and refused to speak to her for several years. And rather than accommodate, back down or apologise, she simply toughed it out until they came round.

Her tenacity of character is a strength which has served her well. She is clearly Joanna in the book – the granddaughter and the one character who reveals a capacity for love, a woman whose marriage is a disaster and whose financial situation rests precariously in the hands of her male relatives. In both cases, it is their instinct for self-preservation that sees them through.

Born Naomi Blanche Thoburn McGaw in 1920, but preferring to be known professionally as 'Jane Hervey', she grew up

in a wealthy upper- middle class family on a country estate in Sussex. The family's fortune had been made by her grand-father on cattle ranches in South America and Australia at the beginning of the century; her mother Pauline Blanche née Tate was Henry Tate's granddaughter. Educated by her nanny at home until she was nine, Naomi then attended the wonder-fully named Heron's Ghyll School for The Daughters of Gentlemen Only, where she was popular and good at gym.

There followed 'finishing' in Paris and 'coming out', the usual pattern for a girl of her time and class. Talking to her about that period of her life, one gets an impression of excite-ment, fun and romance. She met her first love, a writer on the *Daily Sketch*, in Paris when she was eighteen. He was in his early fifties. He helped her with her writing and she began to put together a collection of short stories. They didn't marry because of the age difference.

During the war she did a spell of nursing as well as work for a writer of aircraft recognition books, typing up his manuscripts and acting as both his editor and agent. She met her first husband, a young captain in the Welsh Fusiliers called Peter Jones, in 1941; when they married she was given away by his commanding officer. Six months later Peter was sent to Madagascar and Naomi/Jane never saw him again.

From here things became less fun. The following year, still only 21, she met her second husband, a glamorous Canadian soldier ten years older than her: Stuart Wilder was dazzlingly handsome and charismatic and she was completely smitten. She lived with this compelling man (they would marry in 1948) without realising how miserable he would eventually make her; but it became clear soon after the wedding that he was controlling, manipulative and cruel and she found herself trapped. 'I don't understand why,' Jane Hervey says now, trying to explain it, 'I was always very aggressive except in this one case.' Stuart resented her writing, raiding her desk and burning all her short stories one day when she was out of the house. Determined that he would not win on this score, she rewrote them from memory and hid them under the carpet.

Like many other women in a similar position, she found she had no one to turn to. Her money was tied up in a trust administered by five male trustees, including her father, who refused to believe her side of the story. With no immediate means of supporting herself and her young daughter Mary Jane, who was born in 1949, she could see no way out.

Eventually, after a decade of abuse, she met 'the love of my life' and found the strength to take her husband to court. The Old Bailey judge pronounced Wilder a liar and a cheat and she won the case, giggling with relief in the courtroom as the verdict was read out.

This third marriage – to the writer and businessman George Bowlby – was to be everything her second marriage had not been, although it began in its own storm of controversy. Not only were both parties still married to other people when they fell in love, but George Bowlby was the husband of Jane's niece (ie. the husband of her eldest brother's daughter). Divorce was shocking in itself in the early 1950s but this additional scandal was barely conceivable. In a feud prefiguring what would happen when her book came out, the horrified family closed ranks and took several years to speak to her again.

She and her husband soon had five children between them – George already had a son and a daughter and another son and a daughter were born in the 1950s. Writing took second place to family life and work as they tried their hands at chicken farming in Derbyshire, a second business in Devon, and then moved to Cookham Dene in the heart of the Surrey 'Gin and Jag Belt'. Jane was initially thrilled at the constant parties on offer but now describes their new social life as fairly lurid. Gatherings centred on the local inn, where the unscrupulous publican encouraged an alcohol-fuelled blur of wife-swapping and the fall-out was a series of scandals, divorces and suicides.

It was in Cookham Dene, with three children away at boarding school and a nanny to help with the younger two, that Jane Hervey found the time to look at *Vain Shadow* again. She polished it up and had it accepted and published by Gollancz, a decade after she'd first written it. The dust jacket sported a comment by Elizabeth Jane Howard which read:

'It is most unusual with a first novel to achieve exactly what one set out to do. She displays a remarkable sense of proportion, and writes with the most enviably skilful ease. She should have a dazzling future.'

Reviews were positive and the book was published in America and in Italy the following year.

Jane Hervey is now in her nineties and finds herself in a world of e-books and reading devices, social media and social diversity. At the same time, the 1950s are enjoying a revival – so this is an interesting moment to re-assess her book for its second outing. Yes, it's unashamedly of its time and class. But the things which made it good in the first place remain strong.

When I asked Jane about her influences and interests, she replied, 'Anything family. I always do family'. And her ruthless dissection of family is what the twenty-first century reader will appreciate today.

Jane Hervey's energies and focus were distracted into setting up English Country Cottages (the first holiday rental company of its kind, which flourished during the 1970s, 80s and 90s). And although she followed *Vain Shadow* with a second novel, *Song in the Grass*, and a collection of short stories, these have not been published.

She continues to write, however, and works at her computer in her Norfolk house most days, articulating her dismay at domestic unkindness and the way people submit those closest to them to often invisible and silent cruelties.

Vain Shadow is quietly successful; a steely and accomplished comedy of manners that makes one both laugh with recognition and breathe a sigh of relief that this is not one's own family. It shows us – in the most undramatic but knowing way – how tyranny and casual violence exist in the most civilised of settings; how far – legally, at least – women have come since the 1950s, and how death remains impossible to get right.

Celia Robertson
London, 2014

VAIN SHADOW

THE FIRST DAY

I

'. . . Madam . . . Madam! Nurse asked me to tell you that the Colonel passed away peacefully in his sleep at half past two this morning. . . .'

Dislodged from the security of her drugged darkness, Mrs Winthorpe groped unhappily among the words 'peacefully in his sleep'.

'May I offer my sympathy, Madam?'

'Thank you, Upjohn.'

Peacefully . . . in his sleep. . . .

Never again to have to kiss him goodnight! After fifty-three years of having to kiss him. . . .

What a blessing it was all over! (A blessing for him, she meant, of course!) All over! Sickness. Health. Till death us do part.

Upjohn marched across the thick carpet, pulled back the heavy pink and gold brocade curtains and flung open a window, letting the fresh air and sunlight pour into the bedroom.

Mrs Winthorpe began to wonder whether perhaps, after all, she ought to have asked Nurse to call her when he. . . . A sudden breeze caught the faded pink artificial tulips which stood in a vase on the dressing table, among the heavy silver-backed brushes and hand mirror, photographs of the family and china ornaments; the tulips rustled like dead leaves, calling her immediate attention.

'Don't open the window this morning, Upjohn,' she said quickly, tenderly feeling her neck for rheumatism.

The window snapped shut as sharply, yet almost as silently, as Upjohn's lips.

'And you'd better tell Mr and Mrs Jack and Mr Harry when you call them that the Colonel . . . that it's all over,' Mrs Winthorpe added, as Upjohn was leaving the room.

Outside in the long, oak-panelled corridor, Upjohn paused at the door of the next room and stood, listening. She half-expected to hear *his* cough which for so many years had attacked her when she took in his morning tea. This morning there was no cough. Only silence.

Fancy letting him go alone like that! she said to herself as she walked on along the silent corridor, between the ranks of portraits whose dead eyes seemed to watch her as she passed. Only Nurse and not one of his own with him at the end!

She was quite glad to clatter down the noisy back stairs to the kitchen for the second tray of early morning tea.

She returned with the tray to Mr Jack's room and knocked on the door. There was no reply. She knocked again, more loudly, and went in.

'Good morning, Sir.' She put down the tray and thought again how odd those two heads looked side by side – the young one covered with reddish-gold curls, and the ageing one, quite grey now, with the neat grey beard pointing out over the sheet.

Mr Jack's eyes were slowly opening.

'I'm sorry to say, Sir,' said Upjohn, 'Mrs Winthorpe asked me to tell you that the Colonel passed away peacefully in his sleep at half past two this morning.'

God . . . I'm tired! God! The Old Man's dead!

'Did he ask for me – I mean, for anyone?'

'No, Sir. Nurse said the end was quite peaceful. He just went in his sleep.'

Passed away! Went! Why do these bloody women use such expressions? Can't they just say dead and done with? Jack thought irritably. He turned to Laurine, putting his hand on her bare shoulder and feeling her warmth quiver up his arm.

'Darling,' he said gently. 'It's all over. Father died last night.'

'Oh, poor Father!' Never again would she sit beside Father at the head of the table, terrified in case she might (in spite of Jack's careful coaching) say the wrong thing . . . yet Father had never been cross to her. Perhaps he had even liked her. Her lip trembled, tears pricked her eyes; then she remembered that Jack was the eldest son. He would be rich now. Now they wouldn't have to live just on the money he got for his pictures, which wasn't very much even though he painted so beautifully. Now they would be able to afford a big house, a swimming pool, maids, a car . . . . 'I hope he didn't have any pain . . .' she said.

3

'No, darling. He just died in his sleep.'

'He was always kind to me.' Tears pricked her eyes again: started to spill over and trickle down her cheeks. She quickly felt under her pillow for a handkerchief (one must never show emotion in front of the servants) and moved closer to Jack.

Under cover of the bedclothes, while Upjohn's back was turned as she drew the curtains, Jack put his arm round Laurine, and looking down at her he thought: I hope the Old Boy didn't cut me out as he threatened to when I married her . . . who could blame anyone for marrying her? . . . and what's wrong anyway these days with marrying an actress? . . . especially when they look as lovely offstage as they do on . . . Ridiculous to say I was infatuated! Fifty-one is the prime of life, when a man's judgement is at its soundest.

He bent, with rising eagerness, to kiss Laurine as Upjohn closed the door.

Puffing upstairs for the third time, Upjohn could hear Mr Harry's wireless – an early bird was Mr Harry. Following close upon this daily reflection came a slight sense of shock. The wireless? *This* morning? Then she remembered. Of course. He didn't know yet. How could he?

She knocked, opened the door and sailed into the room – a room filled with music and bright with sunlight which poured in through the wide-open, uncurtained window.

He was sitting up in bed in his blue and white striped pyjamas, crocheting. The bedclothes were pulled comfortably up over his stomach, already full with approaching middle-age, and on his knees rested his pattern which he had fastened with drawing pins to a small pastry board.

He looked up as Upjohn came in and before she had time to open her mouth said: 'Has he gone?'

It spoilt her speech. But she was too fond of Mr Harry to let that matter.

'Yes, Mr Harry, I'm afraid so. At half past two this morning.'

He reached across to turn off the wireless which stood on his bedside table together with his clock, carafe of water and tumbler, his ashtray and his diary.

I needn't have worried, thought Upjohn. You could always depend on Mr Harry to do the right thing.

'It's a blessing, you know, Upjohn. He was very ill and very tired.'

'Oh, yes, Mr Harry.'

'How is my mother? Has she taken it all right?'

'Yes, Sir. She seems quite calm. And I have told Mr Jack.'

There was a slight pause before Mr Harry said: 'I see.'

As she was leaving the room Upjohn said: 'We shall all miss the Colonel, Mr Harry. He's been a good master to us.'

'Thank you, Upjohn. I'm sure you will.'

He answered mechanically, because while he was winding up the ball of cotton and neatly folding his crochet he was telling himself: I must get up at once. There'll be a lot to do. I must see about the death certificate and ring up Brian and Joanna and the aunts and. . . .

He placed the crochet and ball of cotton carefully on the bedside table, pushed the pattern-covered pastry board out of his way and climbed out of bed. He put on his slippers and went over to the dressing table where his belongings were

neatly laid out in a row. He took his spectacles out of their case and put them on. Then he picked up his gold pencil, adjusted the lead and returned to bed. On the bedside table was his diary. He settled it on his knees and began to write:

Monday, June 15th, 1961

1. *Inform Family*
Children
a) Jack (& Laurine) – present
b) Self – present
c) Brian (& Elizabeth) Tel: (Office) Deansgate 86945
                                              (Home) Mere 24
Grandchild(ren)
d) Joanna (and Tony) Tel: (Office) Manchester Central 892
                                              (Home) Poynton 9899
Sisters
e) & f) Aunts Eva & Carrie Tel: Look it up.

He frowned and stopped writing for a moment, pulling gently at his greying moustache.
He began to write again:

2. *The Times*
a) Announcement of Death
b) Obituary . . .

He continued to write energetically, too busy even to light his first cigarette of the day.

II

An hour later Mrs Winthorpe, sitting up in bed playing
patience, heard footsteps coming along the corridor. Bother!
Just as it was going to come out – and the clock patience
hardly ever came out! She hesitated. People might think it
queer to be playing cards (even though it was only patience)
so soon after. . . .

There was a gentle tap on the door.

Mrs Winthorpe leaned down and deftly slid the green
baize-covered board laid out with cards under the bed. She
straightened up, rearranged the frills on her bed jacket and
(just in time) called 'Come in!'

Jack and Laurine came in, hand in hand.

'Good morning.'

''Morning, dear.' Jack bent to kiss her on the forehead,
his free hand pressing hers for a moment, comforting, re-
assuring.

'Good morning, Mother.' Laurine in turn kissed and withdrew. She glanced uneasily from her mother-in-law to Jack,
wondering whether to express sympathy or leave it to him.

To her relief, Jack said: 'Are you all right, Mother? It wasn't
too much of a shock?'

'Oh, no! No. I'm only thankful he didn't have to go on like
that . . . you know. . . .'

'Yes, poor old boy. I somehow felt last night that we
wouldn't see him again.'

She said – she could not help saying – 'You don't think we
ought to have sat up last night, do you?'

'Well, we did all agree – and I think quite rightly – with Harry's suggestion that there should be no deathbed scenes.'

'Yes. . . . Yes, of course we *did* agree, didn't we?' She gave a little sigh of relief.

'Now Mother. . . .' The thing to do was to buck her up so that she had no time to think. '. . . We must ring up Brian and Joanna.'

'Yes, we must ring them up.' A slight frown drew Mrs Winthorpe's well-groomed eyebrows together as she looked at Jack, and the first finger of her right hand picked gently at the skin round the pink polished thumbnail. 'You ring them up, will you, darling? Oh, dear.' She put her hand up to her forehead.

'What is it?'

'Brian will already have left for the office. He catches the 7.55.'

'I suppose we really ought to have got hold of him before he left,' said Jack. His fingers ranged over his beard unhappily, even though it was already brushed trimly into shape.

'Yes, but we didn't know until . . .'

'No, that's right. Of course we didn't.'

'And as a matter of fact, Elizabeth said she would ring up after breakfast to see how Father is – was – so we could leave it until then and ask her to let Brian know.'

'That's a good idea.' Nevertheless, Jack wondered with slight apprehension, would Brian think they ought to have sat up? Old Brian was rather keen on tradition and that sort of thing. . . . Oh, well, Elizabeth would smooth him down. Elizabeth had the gentle touch.

'Joanna was coming this afternoon to see him,' Mrs Winthorpe went on. 'But perhaps you'd better let her know now.'

Jack moved round to the other side of the bed. He picked up the lady with high-piled white silk hair, as smooth and shining white as his mother's own, whose voluminous pink frilled skirts concealed a cream telephone, and lifted the receiver to his ear.

III

'Hello? Joanna?'

'Yes? Who . . . oh, Uncle Jack, is that you?' Her mouth was suddenly dry. Was Grandfather – better?

'Joanna, dear, I don't expect you'll be surprised to hear that it's all over.'

She said automatically: 'No, no, I'm not surprised,' and a great longing surged over her to have seen him, just once more, before he died.

'He didn't regain consciousness after last evening.'

If he had wanted to see her again he would have asked for her. But why should he ask for *her*? She was not one of his sons. She was only his granddaughter, not close to him at all: never had been ever since she began to grow up, to form her own shape, and he had ringed her round with discipline tight as bands round a growing tree. She knew now that she had let this harsh discipline, shaped with knowledge forty years out of date for her growth, turn love into fear, twisting her further and further from him, the only father she had ever known, so

9

that she was unable to turn to him for guidance or help; so that in the end her one overriding aim had been escape from him. Perhaps, if she had only been stronger; perhaps, if he had only stayed as he was when she saw him last, so gentle, so quiet; perhaps, if she had only been able to see him again . . . her throat tightened.

She said harshly: 'Was he in pain?'

'No, no pain at all. He went off to sleep at about half past nine and died at half past two this morning. . . .'

The remainder of her uncle's sentence was lost on the dark plain of Joanna's thoughts. She continued the conversation, his voice and her own running on like thin threads linking the images in her mind:

'I wish I'd seen him again.'

I wonder if his beard was any longer. The first time I've seen him with a beard was the last time I saw him last Wednesday but –

'You couldn't have done anything, Jo, dear. Honestly! It was better not, and you can remember him now as you last saw him.'

– with a little bit of a beard, just a grey silky fluff, so soft it looked. I said: Oh, Grandfather! You've got a beard! And he said: I'm afraid it won't have time to grow very long! And I said: Yes, of course it will! Grow it long like Moses and –

'Uncle Harry said he might get worried if he saw us all rushing round.'

– the bed with his hands lying on the sheet so white and thin. I wish I'd seen him again, just once, though once or twice or seventy times seven, what's the difference? In the end the end must come, and I'd be no closer to him than I ever was.

'He was quite right, of course. And your grandmother has taken it all very calmly and very well.'

Uncle Jack's voice banished the image of grandfather, and Joanna could see her grandmother, stately and beautiful in her immaculate old age.

'Oh, has she?' How does she feel now, after we have talked so often about what she'd do (she wanted a pink bathroom), now that it's really happened?

'She's sitting up in bed looking very perky, bless her!'

Sitting up . . . in her pearls and pale-blue satin bed jacket, not one white curl out of place, the delicate pink-tipped hands smoothing out the sheet in front of her, smoothing out all those creases which to her were so distasteful.

'Oh, not *perky*! Not Grandmother!'

Uncle Jack's laugh sounded rather forced. 'Do you want to have a word with her?'

'Yes, please.' What should she say? What could she say . . . after all that had been said?

'Hallo, darling.'

'Are you all right, Granny?'

'Yes. Yes, thank you. I'm quite all right.'

'It was a blessing really, wasn't it?' What stupid things one says! God, how stupid! Blessing, mercy and we give thee hearty thanks. . . .

'Yes. He was very weak last night.'

'I wish I'd seen him again.'

'Oh, but darling, it's so much better that you didn't! He changed terribly after that last attack on Saturday morning. So much better to remember him as he was when you last saw him.'

– with the soft silvery beard and the pale hands folding the sheet so gently, so patiently, into a little concertina, straightening, pulling out, straightening, then folding and folding again, gently, patiently, not talking, not listening to her, only folding and unfolding, folding and unfolding, the little concertina the only thing that mattered.

'I suppose so.' All the same. . . .

'Are you still coming this afternoon?'

'Yes, please, I'd like to come – maybe there's something I can do.' He would not be there. At least he would . . . but not *him*.

If only it were not too late. If only she could have had one more chance – just one – to talk to him. To say: Grandfather, I have always been afraid of you. Because I was afraid, I tried to escape by marrying Tony – and found an even greater fear, and no love. And when I did find love, with Andrew, I was too frightened to escape from Tony. What shall I do now? Please help me. Please.

IV

'I think we'd better go down, Mother,' said Jack. 'We thought we'd stroll along to the rose garden before breakfast.'

'All right, darling. It's a lovely morning. Oh, dear! There'll be such a lot to see to!'

'Now, don't you worry,' Jack soothed. 'We'll take care of everything.'

'I don't know what I'd do without you. . . .'

As Jack and Laurine left the room, Mrs Winthorpe started to reach under the bed for the patience board. Then she

paused; she straightened herself up with a sigh. There wouldn't be time for any more before Harry came. She'd just get started, and then Harry would come, and the patience wouldn't come out again.

She sank back on the pillows and once more her hands, palms downward, moved sideways apart across the turn-down of the sheet, smoothing it, and returned to rest together in front of her, folded, like the wings of a bird.

Was that *his* cough?

She listened, with her head turned towards the room next door. Her heartbeats quickened. One hand flew to her throat and her fingers caught the seven-strand pearl necklace which Alfred had given her for a wedding present.

No, no, of course it wasn't his cough! How foolish! How could it be? Her heartbeats grew less rapid, slowed down to normal again, although she still held her head cocked, listening, and her fingers tugged gently at the necklace, easing it away from her throat.

When she died, she supposed those pearls really ought to go to the wife of the eldest son. To Laurine. But she had decided to leave them to her granddaughter. After all, Sylvia had been her only daughter, and after her death Joanna had taken her place, brought up as her daughter, far more daughter than granddaughter. Besides, there was Joanna's tall graceful figure – so like her mother's, and her own, too, when she had been young – a perfect setting for pearls. On Laurine pearls would look rather – out of place.

If only Sylvia had not died, she thought, caressing the necklace gently. How lovely she would have looked in pearls

. . . pearls for tears . . . she could see her now on her wedding day, just twenty, so young and tender in white satin and the lace veil which had been her mother's (hers!) and her grandmother's, and was later to be her daughter's (only Joanna wouldn't wear it over her face when she came up the aisle, such a pity, the modern idea, and not nearly as graceful and modest as in the old days) and she had tried so hard not to cry, at least in church, because she had felt quite sure that Dennis was not good enough for Sylvia. And she had been quite right. He'd been so – so offhand with her, even in the little time they were married. And then going off like that and getting married again three months after Sylvia died, leaving Joanna, a tiny baby, to be brought up by her grandparents.

'Disgraceful!' she said aloud, pinching the pearls between finger and thumb. They felt like little frozen teardrops.

Not that she hadn't been glad to have Joanna. How lovely it had been to have a baby in the nursery again after twenty years: old Nannie back and the delicious smell of baby linen airing on the nursery fireguard. It was almost as if Joanna was Sylvia all over again, as if it was her own baby daughter come back to her. Sometimes she got muddled, and thought of Joanna as Sylvia, sometimes even called her Sylvia.

She was so very like Sylvia. The same build, the same laughing blue eyes and warm brown hair that was never quite tidy, the same way of walking with one foot set down quickly and exactly in front of the other like a cat, so that the boys teased her as they teased their sister Sylvia, saying 'Pussyfoot!' and 'Don't slink!' The same proud way of holding her head, the same impatient shaking back of that heavy, brown, never-quite-tidy hair, the same eagerness for life: for making new friends, finding new pets, toys, birds' nests, butterflies, flowers. She remembered once Joanna (or was it Sylvia?) catching hold of one of the big red hot poker flowers which grew in the herbaceous border, clutching the great orange-yellow flame of it with a cry of delight which changed to a cry of pain as the sting of a hidden bee buried itself in the poor, soft little palm. Well – that was life. Things looked so pretty. And then the hidden bee.

Poor Sylvia.

Thank goodness Joanna had married a nice man. One never knew when girls married so young – only twenty, just like Sylvia. But no one could wish for a nicer, better-looking, more charming husband than Tony. Older than Joanna, of course, nearly ten years older, but that was all to the good. She simply couldn't understand why Alfred had never quite taken to him . . . .

The door of the bathroom which separated her room from Alfred's gave a sudden sharp crack. She jumped, and her heart beat faster. She listened, longing for familiar sounds in the silence: the gong for breakfast, Harry's firm knock, Upjohn with her breakfast tray. . . .

She stared at the bathroom door. She imagined it open. Alfred's face appeared round it, cross as usual. He barked good morning at her. So fierce he looked, his white moustache bristling, like a bad-tempered walrus.

Sadly she wondered why he always looked so fierce. And why he barked at her. There he would sit in his old brown armchair in the hall, with his feet up on *her* fireside stool,

wearing out the top of it which she had worked so carefully in Jacobean tapestry. And perhaps she would make some remark, quite a harmless remark (about the weather, perhaps, or the news) and he would put down one of those dreadful detective stories he was always reading and bark at her. 'What?' he would say – oh, it was like being shot at! – 'What?' – as though she had no right to speak!

She wished her heart would stop beating so fast and the engine stop knocking in her head. Dr James said that it was palpitations, caused by a tired heart. But that wasn't true. They were not caused by a tired heart: they were caused by Alfred. Glaring at her; barking at her; grumbling at her . . . for years and years, almost from their very wedding day. Why? *Why?*

A sudden knock startled her. Harry! He always walked so quietly. One never heard a sound; and then, suddenly, there he was.

As she reached up to kiss him it struck her that they would live together now, now that she was a – a widow. It had always been understood that they should live together if anything happened to Father. She did hope Harry would not get cross with her.

'Well . . .' she hesitated.

She glanced at the bathroom door. The thought arrived in her mind that she must remove Alfred's bath towel now. It had hung there for so many years, and he always would insist upon having a white towel which quite spoilt the effect of her peach ones. And he wouldn't allow her to have that horrid old white bath replaced, even though she had offered to pay for a new peach one herself out of her own money. She did so want a peach bath and basin. Not pink. Peach! She hoped Harry would agree. Supposing he didn't approve of peach?

'It's a blessing it's all over . . .' she said tentatively. 'It is a release for him.'

'Yes.' Harry walked across to the window and stood looking out. The terrace with slender leaden urns standing along the low grey stone wall like sentinels capped with red geraniums: the rose garden, kept not quite up to pre-war standards, which with its riot of colour and growth seemed today almost sacrilegiously beautiful: the field beyond, which had once been a deer park and was now grazing for a neighbour's cattle: the distant Derbyshire peaks: all this formed the backdrop to his vision of the recumbent figure in the next room, sleeping into death in the muffled light with Nurse, white-aproned and capped with white wings, bending angel-like above the bed: listening: watching; waiting.

He returned to his mother's bedside, comforted by his vision. 'I feel sure the end was quite peaceful.'

'Oh, yes, quite. He never regained consciousness, you know. Of course Dr James said last night that he might not,' she added, almost to herself.

'I know.' The still figure on the bed faded from Harry's mind, replaced by images of ringing up the rest of the family, seeing about the funeral arrangements, doing everything that there was to be done . . . .

'What about Brian and Joanna?' he asked.

'Jack rang Joanna. She was coming this afternoon, anyway. We didn't ring Brian because he would have already left for the office. It's rather awkward, really. . . .'

'Why?'

'Well . . . it's a pity we didn't catch him before he left.'

'But how could we? Doesn't he catch the 7.55?'

'Yes, he does. But he . . . Father died at half past two this morning.'

'Well, but look here, Mother.' Bother! Why must she upset his vision! But steady now. Her generation had always revered a deathbed and it was only natural that she might be worried that no one had been with Father when he died. 'You know,' he said gently, 'we *did* all agree that no one was to be called unless he particularly asked for them.'

'Oh, I know, I know. Elizabeth is ringing up at breakfast time so we can ask her to let Brian know. But I just thought it was rather a pity we didn't think to ask Nurse to tell us . . . at once . . . we could have caught Brian before he left then.'

He kept his voice gentle. 'I don't see that that was really necessary. And it's no good thinking of it now, I'm afraid.'

'No, I suppose not. . . .' She began to pick again at the dry skin round her thumbnail. 'But perhaps we ought to have thought of it last night and made arrangements . . . although we weren't *quite* sure he was going to . . .'

'Exactly!' Harry interrupted her; and this time, warned by the faintest note of impatience which she thought she detected in his voice, Mrs Winthorpe said no more.

The silence in the room was broken only by the quick, gentle, almost inaudible tick-tick of the picking finger. Then Harry, too, started to pick at his thumb and the pizzicato duet continued for a few moments unimpeded.

Like a handful of pebbles into a pool, the thought of the

tenants splashed into Harry's mind, and he said: 'What about letting the people on the estate know?' He reached into his pocket for his diary.

'Oh . . . I hadn't thought . . . perhaps Jack ought to go round and tell them?'

'Is that really necessary?'

'Oh. Well . . . what do you suggest?'

'Obviously Upjohn will have told everyone in the house, and all we've got to do is to let the people in the cottages know. I'll send out a message for Brown when he comes in with the vegetables and he can tell Tommy to go round with notes to the cottages. I'll write them out after breakfast.'

'Thank you, darling. But don't you think perhaps . . . Jack might like to write them? After all, he is the eldest. . . .'

He sighed. He knew Jack was the eldest. But he himself had given up a promising career in an estate agent's, with an almost certain chance of a partnership, in order to manage Father's two thousand acres. He had been Father's right-hand man. Father had depended upon him absolutely.

'Very well,' he said. 'I merely thought that as I have always lived here and managed Father's estate, and Jack only comes once or twice a year, it might be better if *I* did it.'

'I see. . . .' Mrs Winthorpe let her voice fade out. She hated arguments. She would leave them to sort it out between them. 'What about the – the funeral?' she asked.

'We can start making arrangements after breakfast. I've made out a list. You needn't worry. I'll see to everything.'

'Oh, thank you, Harry.' Harry *was* efficient! Jack was very willing; and very kind; but not *quite* so capable.

Upjohn brought in Mrs Winthorpe's breakfast.

'Well, Mother,' said Harry, 'I'll be going down.'

He paused until Upjohn had left the room. When they were alone once more he continued: 'I'll have a word with Jack about letting the tenants know, and we'll go ahead with making plans for the funeral.'

Today's Monday, he said to himself, and it's warm weather. His fingers tapped one after another against his loose grey linen jacket as he counted the days.

'Thursday, I should think,' he said.

'Yes,' replied Mrs Winthorpe, then her voice rose in sudden distress as she called: 'Upjohn! Oh, Upjohn! Bother. She's gone. And she's forgotten the cream *again*. Would you mind telling her when you go down, Harry? She's been getting very careless lately, I'm afraid.'

'All right, I'll tell her.' From the doorway he said: 'She's had a lot of extra work to do recently, you know.'

He closed the door gently.

V

Harry walked along the corridor, his half-closed fists held a little away from his body and moving in slow, firm semicircles alternately backwards and forwards, sculling his portly figure along the stream of his intent direction. As he walked, he reviewed the already formed curriculum in his mind.

Halfway along the corridor he paused; he turned his head back over his shoulder. Funny, he said to himself, I never

20

even thought about going in to say good morning to Father, although I've done it every morning up till now. Never missed it until I'd already passed his door.

He almost felt that he should go back along the corridor again in order to pass the closed door and *miss* knocking on it and going in to say good morning. Then he shrugged, turned his face towards the wide staircase and went sculling forwards, his mind busy again with his curriculum, checking, modifying, augmenting.

As he descended heavily into the hall, the big oak front door creaked open and Jack and Laurine came in. Laurine's cotton frock made a bright splash of colour against the dark oak panelling.

Surely she could have found something a little less garish for this morning, Harry thought, and he greeted her coldly.

'Good morning!' Laurine gave Harry her usual half-mocking, half-coquettish bow, but this morning her gay smile was subdued. She stood still, balancing on the high, thin heels which she knew he considered ridiculous, clasping her hands behind her back so that her small pointed breasts were thrown into prominence. Harry averted his eyes.

'Morning,' said Jack.

The three of them looked at one another.

'Well . . .' said Jack. Silence fell again; lengthened; began to be embarrassing.

Upjohn came in to sound the gong.

She bent to pick up the padded stick and raised it towards the brass disc which hung like a big, bright medal below the stuffed head of a stag shot by Father at Loch Earn in 1924.

Harry said quickly: 'It's all right, Upjohn. We're all here. There's no need to ring it this morning.'

'No need at all!' Jack echoed.

That dreadful, deafening outbreak of noise – fit to awaken the dead!

'I don't think Nurse is down yet, Sir.' Upjohn was still holding the stick uplifted, threatening the gong below the nose of the offended stag.

Harry and Jack looked at each other: *ought* we to ring the gong this morning?

'Well . . . ring it very gently, then, Upjohn,' Harry said at last, and Jack chimed in, 'Yes, very gently.'

'Of course, Sir.'

Nevertheless, Laurine put her hands over her ears and skipped quickly on ahead into the dining room before the noise could catch her.

She called out: 'Nurse is here already!'

Upjohn lowered the stick and replaced it gently underneath the gong.

'I'm sorry,' she said. 'I didn't know Nurse was in the dining room. I didn't come through that way.'

'That's quite all right, Upjohn,' said Jack, getting it in quickly, before Harry.

'Upjohn, would you mind taking up Mrs Winthorpe's cream,' said Harry, suddenly remembering. 'It wasn't on the tray.'

With his hands deep in his pockets, Jack strode after Laurine into the dining room, Harry sculling along behind him.

As she made her way to the long, mahogany table, the surface of which had acquired a lightened gleam throughout countless summers of sunlight and the busy polishing of countless servants until it looked like rich, melted honey, Laurine thought how wonderful it would have been if only, as one read in books, this lovely great house could have been handed down from father to eldest son – from Father to Jack, from Jack to his son, *their* son – if only they could have one!

The house, built three hundred years ago, of stone and slate, stood halfway up a hill, facing undisturbed the fierce gales that from time to time attacked it from the valley, battering at its windows and tearing at the old wisteria which twisted across the front of it like a long, grey snake.

One approached the house from the other side, the sheltered side, up a quarter-mile drive along an avenue of elm trees, passing into the cobbled courtyard between two stone pillars supporting black and gold painted wrought-iron gates which stood permanently open. The oak front door, iron-studded, and with hinges of wrought iron, gave entrance to the house for the family and visitors; a smaller edition, the back door, which also opened onto the courtyard, admitted servants and tradesmen. Cut into the stone lintels over both doors, but larger over the front door, was the Winthorpe family crest and the Winthorpe family motto. Beside the front door stood the old mounting-stone, the top of it velvety with green and golden moss, and beside the back door a stone drinking trough.

The drive swept round the corner of the house to the garages and stables. The clock tower rose above the stables.

Its clock had been removed because it struck the hour too loudly, leaving a staring round hole like a ravaged eye socket.

From the stables a gravel path led between dark yew hedges clipped into peacocks, ships, cockerels, past the blackened ruins of the old, burnt-down chapel, past the tennis courts and the swimming pool to the wrought-iron gates which led into the walled kitchen garden. Only a quarter of its two acres, neatly dissected by gravel paths, was now in use, neatly laid out with vegetables and soft fruit; the rest was put down to grass and kept well scythed. And only one of the five greenhouses was now filled with grapes, peaches, tomatoes; the others, although tidily maintained, were empty.

Another pair of wrought-iron gates led out of the kitchen garden, through the orchard and into the woods which stretched upwards, covering the hillside behind the house until they suddenly ejected one from their shadows onto the flat bleak stretches of the grouse moors.

Two thousand acres. Two *thousand*! Laurine thought. To be mistress of all this estate, and of all the people who served it! People bowing, and calling her madam. . . .

'Good morning, Nurse,' she said, smiling at Nurse graciously (she was the lady of the house, charming, cultured).

Nurse stood by the solid mahogany sideboard waiting her turn for the eggs and bacon. She shifted her weight from one foot to the other, and the graciousness of Laurine was thrown away upon her. She was tired and she was hungry. Her greeting was even more brusque than usual.

'Eggs and bacon, Laurine?' Harry took the top off the oval blue dish on the electric heater.

The smell was delicious but Laurine, shaking her head vigorously, patted her stomach: 'Think of my figure!'

Harry had not the faintest desire to think of Laurine's figure.

'Ridiculous!' he grunted. 'All the banting you girls do nowadays!'

Laurine beamed at him. He might sound grumpy sometimes, but he was a sweet old thing really.

As she went to take her place at the table, she surreptitiously looked to see whether by any chance Upjohn might have put her at the foot of the table now that her husband had the right to sit at the head. But Mrs Winthorpe's armchair was pushed in close to the table, the place unlaid, and Laurine's own place was, as usual, next to Jack.

She sat down, unfolded her table napkin ('Don't for heaven's sake call it a serviette!'), shook it discreetly and laid it tidily across her knees.

Nurse came to the table with a plateful of eggs and bacon.

Jack turned to her. 'You must be very tired,' he said, with immense concern. 'I do hope you managed all right? You could always have come for one of us, you know.'

Harry looked up sharply. There it was again – just like Mother – what was the use of agreeing not to sit up if they were all going to start feeling guilty about it now?

'I managed all right, thank you,' Nurse said stiffly. It was not the first time she had been alone with someone while they were dying. No doubt it would not be the last. Didn't they think her capable?

Harry went over to the sideboard to fetch an egg specially

boiled for him. He felt his irritation mounting. Thank goodness, anyway, for boiled eggs; fried things always gave him
indigestion, and that, on top of everything else, really would
have been *too* much.

'Did you manage to get some sleep?' asked Jack, leaning
again towards Nurse solicitously. Take a kindly interest; they
appreciated it. Buxom wench!

'I had forty winks.'

Harry sat down, carefully placing his boiled egg on the
table in front of him. He removed its blue woollen cosy,
tapped with his knife gently round the egg, an accurate three-
quarters of an inch from the top, then neatly decapitated it.
The operation over, he sat back with a sigh of relief and
happily regarded the egg, opened and inviting. Just right.
Four minutes exactly, by the look of it. He was feeling better
already.

'I think you've been wonderful with him,' Jack said to
Nurse. 'Don't you, darling?' he turned to Laurine.

'Oh, yes. Oh, yes, of course. I do, certainly!'

'He was a very good patient.' Nurse felt suddenly generous. 'He never grumbled, you know, poor old gentleman. He
was always so grateful for everything I did and so anxious not
to be any trouble.'

They all paused to regard, through Nurse's eyes, the old
man whom alive they had known fierce, intolerant, ever-
battling, consecrated now in dying, humble and saintly. Which
was the true man: which the shadow?

Harry said cautiously: 'Of course, he wasn't in any pain at
the end, was he, Nurse?'

'Oh, no. He had morphia, you know.'

'Yes. I just wanted to make sure.' Harry got up and went to the sideboard to fetch his second egg.

Jack glanced at his broad grey back, and his gaze returning to the table was arrested by the vision of Nurse buttering her fourth scone. God, these people! How they ate! No wonder they were fat! He looked at Laurine. She didn't eat too much; although she wasn't too thin. Nicely covered. In the right places.

Harry came back to the table with his second egg and proceeded to deal with it in the same way as he had the first. Tap, tap, tap.

Nurse pushed back her chair and got to her feet, smoothing down her apron and adjusting her broad starched belt.

'Well,' she said, when she had swallowed the last mouthful of scone, 'I must get back to my . . .'

Jack turned quickly towards her. Harry lifted his head, startled, his hand holding the carefully poised knife arrested in mid-air. Laurine held her breath. They all waited, suspended: surely she wasn't going to say, as she had said every other morning in just that very tone of cheerfulness assumed for the benefit of next-of-kin: 'I must get back to my patient'?

But she concluded: '. . . to my packing' and they relaxed.

As soon as Nurse had left the room Jack said: 'We'll have to start making funeral arrangements.'

'Yes.' Harry levelled his knife at his egg. 'Thursday, I thought . . . oh, blast!' With a swift sweep of the knife he had decapitated the egg. A stream of almost-liquid white poured out of the shell, trickling down the sides of the egg cup. 'This

egg's not properly done! Why on earth can't they be consistent, and do it properly? They know I like it *exactly* four minutes. Surely they can tell the time?'

He got up and stalked across to the fireplace to press the bell, hard and long, until it began to hurt the tip of his finger. Suddenly conscious that he would never do such a thing as a rule, he snatched his hand away and returned to the table. 'Well, anyway . . . Thursday. Do you agree?'

'Yes, I do indeed,' said Jack. 'We can get an announcement off to *The Times* today.'

'And while we're about it,' Harry went on, 'Mother thought *you* ought to write the notes for the tenants.'

Of course I ought! Jack thought indignantly. 'Yes,' he said. 'That would be an idea.'

'Tommy Brown can take them round. He's usually indoors out of sight, but he does do occasional jobs and errands still.'

'Poor devil! Fancy still being alive in that condition! Do you remember how he used to scare us when we were children?'

Harry saw Tommy Brown appear from behind the high wall which surrounded the kitchen garden, muttering and signalling; beneath the low wrinkled forehead frothed with down, his dark Mongolian eyes peered, mournful with age-old sorrow at ever-striving and ever-failing to make himself understood. He really ought to have insisted on Tommy being put away years ago, Harry thought. But he hadn't the heart. He pushed the memory away from him.

'I'll compose the notice for *The Times*,' he said. 'I wonder if we should put "Dearly beloved husband of . . ."'

'Well, hardly dearly *beloved* . . .' said Jack. He paused. They could hear Upjohn coming through the pantry. The twin shadows of her feet appeared in the gap beneath the serving room door.

'Just "husband of", I should think,' he concluded hurriedly as the swing-door opened and Upjohn came in.

Her face registered slight affront, which she had underlined by not answering the bell *immediately* because that bell had been pressed very hard and very long indeed.

'Oh, Upjohn, this egg!' Harry held it up in its cup, oozing, dripping, slowly congealing. 'It's not done enough. Would you ask Mrs Burton to boil me another one, and this time for *exactly* four minutes, please.'

Laurine looked down at the tablecloth – crocheted by Harry – and smiled.

Upjohn went off, taking with her the discarded egg. Fancy her Mr Harry pressing the bell in that manner!

Harry looked after her doubtfully, then sat back in his seat to await his egg. His raised eyes encountered the stern gaze of Father who watched him from the gilt frame hanging above the sideboard. He suddenly remembered Brian and Joanna flipping butterballs at that portrait, one on the end of the nose counting as a bullseye. There had been that dreadful occasion not so very long ago – although it must have been five years at least, because Joanna was still at school, he remembered – when Joanna had scored a bull'seye just a second or so before Father came into breakfast, ten minutes late as usual because he saw to his mail first, and no one had had time to pick the butterball off. And there they had to sit,

all through breakfast, on tenterhooks lest Father should happen to look above the sideboard and see himself with a butterball on the end of his nose. Brian ought never to have encouraged Joanna in such pranks. Harry had spoken to him about it at the time.

'I can't think why you always knock the tops off those things,' said Jack. 'If you peel the shell at the top, the way I do, you can tell before you've got very far whether it's properly cooked or not. And if it isn't, you can send the same egg back to be done a bit more instead of wasting it.'

'Quite,' said Harry. Suddenly he exploded. 'But I'd rather do it *my* way! I don't like getting bits of broken shell in my mouth just for the sake of one egg.' There. He felt better after that. What with Mother's and Jack's concern about not sitting up, and then that dratted egg, things had been getting quite out of hand. Relieved, his balance restored, he felt briskly in his pocket for his diary and gold pencil.

'Now look here,' he said. 'Don't you think it would be a good thing if we ran through a list of the things we've got to do today? I've already made one out, but there's just a chance that you might be able to think of something I may have missed.'

'That's an idea,' said Jack, thinking with returning indignation that of course there was a chance – a very good chance.

Harry placed the diary open on the table in front of him and paused for a moment, holding the top of his pencil against his front teeth. He started to read aloud.

'One,' he read. 'Inform family. Elizabeth's going to be asked to tell Brian. . . .' He put a tick in his diary. 'Telephone

Joanna – that's been done.' He put another tick. 'Aunt Eva and Aunt Carrie – I'll see to them after breakfast. Two, announcement and obituary for *The Times*. Three, ring up the undertaker. . . .' He hesitated, then said: 'I think we ought to get him taken down to the funeral parlour, don't you?'

'I don't really know.' Jack felt rather embarrassed. 'Is that the usual form?'

'I think that would be the best arrangement. Better than keeping him here until Thursday (always supposing we can arrange the funeral for Thursday). He can't very well lie in state in the drawing room, say, can he?'

'Oh, Lord, no!'

'Four, go and see old Mr Russell about the funeral arrange-ments. We'd better do that together this morning. Find out from Mother what sort of music she wants and so on and get it all fixed up. "Sheep May Safely Graze" is a lovely thing.'

'Never heard of it.' Jack pushed his chair away from the table and, leaning back, crossed his legs comfortably. He took a long pull at his cigarette and regarded Harry through the clouds of smoke. Harry was in his element. His greying head, with hair still as thick and curly as it had been when he was a boy, was bent earnestly over his diary. Jack was reminded of their schooldays and the numerous clubs they used to form, himself, Harry and Brian – somehow, although Harry was two years younger than himself, it had always seemed to be Harry who was president.

Harry overlooked Jack's ignorance of music. 'Five,' he continued. 'Go and see Mr Trent about the will.'

Jack sat upright. 'Oh, yes?' He leaned forward.

'Brian and I will do that when he gets here. As you know, he and I are the sole executors.' Harry's firm voice set Jack back in his chair again.

'Yes, I know.' Jack glanced at Laurine, then back again to Harry. 'Still, there shouldn't be any difficulty over it, should there?' he appealed. 'I mean . . . it ought to be quite straight-forward, oughtn't it?'

Upjohn came in with Harry's egg.

Irritably, Jack shifted his position. *Hell!* She *would* inter-rupt!

'Thank you, Upjohn.' Harry, pleased at the arrival of this egg, which he knew could be trusted after his gentle rebuke, smiled at her.

How these old girls lap it up! thought Jack, watching Up-john's grim face break into a simper for Harry. Go on, you silly old thing! he wanted to say. Leave us alone! He was scarcely able to hide his eagerness to press Harry for reassurance. It was as though they were back in boyhood, and he had been naughty and wanted Harry to find out for him whether it was safe for him to come out now or whether he was still in disgrace.

His foot moved up and down, beating the air in exasper-ation. He sniffed loudly and his thumb and forefinger picked at the rim of his nostril.

Laurine looked at him. That habit was the one thing about which *she* was allowed to correct *him*. She gave him a sharp kick under the table. He frowned at her and jerked his leg away. Nevertheless, he dropped the offending hand and took another cigarette from the open box on the table, waiting for

Upjohn to leave the room. As the door closed behind her, he returned to the attack.

'After all, it's quite straightforward . . . isn't it?'

'What?'

'The will.'

But Harry was once more engrossed in the delicate operation which he was about to perform upon his third egg. 'I suppose so,' he said vaguely. 'I really don't know, though. I'm only an executor.'

Jack grunted with frustration. There was obviously nothing to be got out of Harry. Bloody old oyster. He took hold of Laurine's hand.

'Come on, darling,' he said, hiding, with an effort, his annoyance. 'We must get cracking. We'll leave Harry to his egg.'

Harry did not look up. He was tapping carefully round his egg.

Halfway across the room Jack stopped. His annoyance was overcome by the thought that Laurine had no mourning, and he had no car.

'Oh, I say, Harry . . .' he said. 'This child . . .' he pulled and swung at Laurine's arm, smiling at her fondly, '. . . hasn't a thing to wear that isn't all colours of the rainbow!'

She wouldn't have, thought Harry.

'Would you mind very much running us into town this morning?'

'Very well.' Harry drew his lips together, frowned, and bent once more over his egg. One swift blow! Then his lips and eyebrows relaxed. It was beautifully done. Four minutes exactly!

They'd been quite right not to sit up. After all, Father would have been the last person to condone such sentimentality.

VI

Joanna slowed the car as she drove up the familiar drive to Otterley Hall. She knew like old friends every one of those tall, rook-haunted elms in the avenue – how many times had she played hide-and-seek in them, and not so very long ago – and there was the quaint stone shrine built three centuries ago by the Catholic family who had built Otterley, standing at the edge of the drive, halfway up, the grey, mossed stones rising to an arch over the niche in which hung the sad little figure of Christ.

How would the house be now, she wondered. Now – without *him*.

No longer to hear that cough. Nor the slow, heavy, rhythmical tap of his walking stick. Not to smell the cigarette smoke pouring out of the hall, advertising his presence within, sitting in that old brown chair smoking cigarette after cigarette down to half an inch of smouldering ash in the long black holder; then tipping the ash gently into an ashtray and groping without looking up among the things on his smoking table for yet another cigarette from the polished oak box which he himself had made; fitting it into the holder, the sudden spurt and flash of the big table lighter; and then the smoke once more puffed out silently, interminably, into the overladen room.

34

As she stood outside the heavy front door she felt the old, familiar sense of fear – unreasonable now. Nevertheless, she hesitated, listening. No. This time there could be no cough. No heavy footsteps, no thud of a stick. Yet still she pushed the door open gently, listening for the sounds she would not hear, and walked softly past the stuffed grizzly bear with its toothy grin and unnaturally pink tongue, which stood on its hind-legs and held out a tray for visiting cards.

The hall was the same. Exactly the same. The same faded and in places threadbare tapestries all but covering the oak-panelled walls, the same old ceiling barred with dark oak beams and dappled brown and yellow with years of smoke from cigars, cigarettes, pipes, the fire. There was no fire today, and the iron dogs stood empty beneath the great wooden overmantel which bore the carved, interlaced names Alfred-Mary, like the carved names of any young couple on any tree anywhere. Above and to each side of the fireplace were the stark skulls, each bearing a veritable tree of antlers, of moose shot by Grandfather in Canada. Those skulls had once been covered with soft, creamy hair which as a child Joanna had loved to touch while she looked up into the big dark glass eyes, making believe she could see something move in them, something alive. Then moth had got into the hair and, rather than part with his trophies, Grandfather had had them stripped, the eyes removed and, worst of all, the skulls painted white, ghastly, glaring white, so that they lit out viciously into the sombre room.

Beneath one of the glaring skulls, beside the fire, stood the chair – his chair.

Joanna was suddenly and with horror surprised not to see him sitting there, smoke ringing a halo round his white head.

On the table beside his chair stood a bottle of gin. Her feeling of horror intensified. Gin! On *his* table, beside *his* chair! She wanted to snatch it up and hide it quickly, quickly – while there was still time. Fancy having drinks in the house before a meal – when he'd always maintained alcohol should only be drunk with a meal – and before lunch at that!

A low murmur of conversation reached her. She hesitated for a moment, then walked across the hall and opened the door into the drawing room, passing from darkness to lightness, to a creamy room filled with delicate furniture of pale honey-coloured woods, materials of soft blues and golds, little cushions, mats, ornaments – a feminine room, her grandmother's room.

There they were – her grandmother, Uncle Jack, Uncle Harry, Laurine, all seated in a semi-circle round the grate in which silver-painted fir cones were piled high against a fan of pink, pleated paper. Where, she wondered, were Uncle Brian and Aunt Elizabeth?

The polite flurry of welcome over, a momentary hush fell on the group after it had resettled to include Joanna.

Harry broke it. 'We've spent the whole morning making the arrangements for Thursday, Joanna. The funeral will be at two-thirty in the afternoon.'

'You'd better come on Wednesday for the night, you and Tony,' said Mrs Winthorpe. 'Or come tomorrow, if you'd rather. How is Tony?'

'Very well, thank you,' Joanna replied. But she didn't want Tony here, neither in the flesh nor in her thoughts. She stood up and walked away from him, over to the open window where she could breathe the mild sweet scent of wisteria and concentrate on it and the roses and the green fields beyond sloping down to the valley, concentrate until they closed around Tony and drove him out of existence.

What a day to die! she thought. All this scent, colour, sound – and to be no more a part of it!

The dark, blurred body of a bumble bee hovered above the mauve trusses of blossom, strumming and scribbling an intricate pattern which seemed obscure and without end until it dashed a sudden purposeful oblique line through the blue sky and vanished on its intent mission. She envied its sudden strength of purpose. Andrew! she thought. And the name was like a pain in her heart.

'Joanna, why don't you sit down?'

Her grandmother's voice flung round Joanna like a thin but tenacious noose, and she jerked her shoulders in exasperation.

Mrs Winthorpe noted the sudden movement uneasily. There had been something disturbing about Joanna lately, something which she couldn't quite understand. A sort of discontentment, a nervousness. Though why should she be discontented? How could she be, with a husband like Tony? So charming. So good-looking, with that dark hair winging back at the sides and neat moustache. And such handsome blue eyes! She would have liked a husband like that herself. Surely it would be impossible not to be happy with a husband like that?

'Joanna!'

'Yes, Granny?'

'Do come and sit down, darling. You look worn out already!'

Joanna sighed and walked back to the sofa. Yes, she was tired. Her head ached, and there seemed to be an invisible plaster between her eyebrows, crinkling up the skin. She put up her hand to smooth it away.

'I am tired,' she admitted. 'I didn't sleep well last night. Can I go to your room and get an aspirin?' Then she remembered that she would have to pass Grandfather's door. 'Oh, no,' she added quickly. 'I don't think I'll bother after all, just now.'

'Well, do if you want to, darling . . .'

'No, it's all right, thanks. Really. Where's Uncle Brian?'

'He'll be here any moment now. He had one or two things to sort out at the office, then he was coming straight here,' said Harry. 'It was rather awkward having the funeral on Thursday,' he went on, ignoring Joanna's look of surprise – he was quite capable of proceeding with arrangements in Brian's absence. 'Mr Russell had a church bazaar that afternoon. He had to cancel it, of course. We didn't want to wait until Friday.'

'It's such a pity the organist's so bad,' said Mrs Winthorpe. 'Miss Dale is really too old. And, of course, there's no choir.'

'Couldn't you have it at Ancaster church?' Joanna suggested. 'Then Mr Legge would be taking the service, and he's so much better than poor old Mr Russell, isn't he?'

'Oh, *no*!' Mrs Winthorpe exclaimed in a shocked voice. 'Grandfather doesn't like Mr Legge!'

It was just as though Grandfather was still there, perhaps always would be there, somewhere . . . waiting to pounce. Joanna remembered the bottle of gin on his table; she wondered how they dared.

'Anyway,' said Harry. 'It's all arranged now. We went to see Mr Russell this morning. We've chosen the music and the hymn. It'll all be very simple.'

'"Sheep may safely graze!"' said Jack, suddenly remembering.

Harry glanced at him, then turned to Joanna.

'I suppose you don't want to see him, do you?'

'See who?'

'Father.'

'*See* him?' Joanna recoiled from the vision of the fierce impatient old man become suddenly and forever still and silent.

'No, I don't,' she said. 'I'd rather remember him when he was alive.' Or rather, she corrected herself, when he was, even though she had not at the time fully realised it, dying. She did not want to remember him when he had been fierce, unapproachably fenced about by his fierceness. She did not want to remember her fear. Suddenly she saw herself walking down the aisle on his arm, in her white satin wedding dress and her grandmother's borrowed pearls and lace veil, and she remembered the feeling which had filled her as he gave her to Tony: the feeling had been, above all else, one of deliverance.

'Yes,' said Jack, after passing his hand over the top of his head – his hair wasn't getting thin, was it? 'That's what we all felt.' He sniffed.

'They're coming for him this afternoon,' Harry remarked. There was almost a smile on his face, a rejoicing at arrangements satisfactorily made with the certainty that they would be equally satisfactorily carried out.

'Wrightson's,' he continued, explaining in answer to Joanna's look of bewilderment.

'Who are Wrightson's?'

'Undertakers.'

'But why are they coming *for* him?'

'To take him away. To the funeral parlour. He'll stay there until Thursday.'

Mrs Winthorpe busied herself with the folds of her dress.

'But can't he stay here?' Joanna protested. 'After all, it is his own home.'

'We can hardly have him lying in state here, can we?' said Harry, with great and obvious patience. Really, Joanna was being very trying. Although she at least hadn't mentioned their not sitting up. But then she wouldn't: not her generation.

'Well, I don't know. . . .' Joanna began to retreat from Harry's imminent annoyance. 'It's nothing to do with me, I suppose. . . .'

She heard echoes of the old man's orders to all who displeased him to 'stay away from here if you can't behave', and the inevitable finale of many times repeated tales of scoundrels who had 'never come here again'. Now he himself was going to be bundled out of his own house, his turn had come at last: he was not even going to be allowed these few final hours to rest in peace in the home which had been his for eighty-two years.

Perhaps it was no more than he deserved. But she still could not help remembering him at the last, meek, humble and perhaps afraid, beaten by the one situation he could never master; when all his rage and all his power could not aid him; when he must do as he was told, go where he was sent . . . .

'Couldn't he stay in his bedroom?' she asked gently.

'Oh, Joanna! The arrangements have all been made now!' Harry's patience broke down, but he quickly stifled his annoyance because it was unseemly. 'Please don't interfere,' he added, but as a request rather than an order.

Mrs Winthorpe stood up. 'I'm just going to call Nurse,' she said. 'She'll be going very soon. I must thank her for all she's done.'

At the door she paused. 'Do you know,' she said to Joanna in an awed voice, 'I found her sitting in *his* chair before lunch!'

Joanna was shocked. It was almost like sitting on *him*.

'Yes! Most odd, I thought it,' said Mrs Winthorpe as she opened the door. She turned back, shook her head and frowned: 'Most tactless!'

The door closed behind her.

Jack came over to sit on the vacant space on the sofa between Joanna and Laurine, putting his arm round Laurine.

'All right, darling?' he said to her.

Then he turned to Joanna. 'Listen, Joanna,' he spoke confidentially, leaning his head towards her. 'We want to get Mother out of the way when the . . . when they come for him. Do you think you could keep her in the hall, or something? Talk to her about something and keep her there?'

'I should think so. I could try. But she'll probably hear them coming downstairs. . . .' One, two; one, two; one, two. Steady round the corner now! Supposing they dropped him? Bang! She shivered.

'No, we thought he could go down in the luggage lift.'

'In the *luggage* lift? Oh, my God, no! That's too much!' Her voice rose, cracked a little, and Jack, embarrassed, glanced at Harry, who said quickly: 'We weren't altogether happy about it, but it seemed the best . . .'

'And Father is so very heavy,' said Laurine.

'But the back stairs! The luggage lift! What a way to go out of your own house! Oh, I think it's awful! Awful!' Joanna jumped up from the sofa but even as she began to walk across the room she started to feel ashamed of her outburst which had made those worried faces even more worried. After all, what did the luggage lift matter now? It didn't – except as an excuse to explode some of the tension inside her, at the core of which was Tony.

'Now, now, Joanna,' Jack soothed. 'Don't get in a state. After all, it was only a suggestion.'

'It seemed the best way to avoid Mother knowing,' Harry added.

'But she knows they're coming for him, because you've just been talking about it in front of her.'

'I know, I know!' Jack started to pick at his nose and Joanna, waiting for his reply, waited also for the inevitable gentle slap from Laurine. 'But we didn't want it to be too obvious,' he went on. 'Sort of tone it down a bit, you know . . . .' The slap came: he jumped and frowned.

Joanna felt hysterical giggles threatening her and in defence concentrated upon the thought of the luggage lift, trying to disapprove of it.

'Anyway, perhaps it would not be *quite* the thing.' Jack glanced at Harry, after imprisoning and squeezing Laurine's hand and returning it to her. 'Don't you agree?'

Harry nodded slowly. Then he said to Joanna: 'The van will be coming for him between three-thirty and four o'clock.'

Van? A small one – bright green – rattled out of her mind down the drive, its half-open doors tied together with string, the end of the coffin sticking out between them.

'Van?'

'The undertaker's van,' Harry explained with a frown. Really, what *was* the matter with Joanna?

'Is it green?'

'*Green!*' Was she mad?

'You called it a van,' she explained, inadequately she realised (for after all there were orange, blue, red, almost any-coloured vans as well as green ones). Harry began: 'Well, I still fail to see what you're . . .' Then Jack interrupted helpfully: 'The undertaker's van is a sort of hearse, I believe.'

'Oh, I see!' And with relief she saw it, this time large and black and dignified, sailing smoothly down the drive, silver handles on doors which were decently closed.

'I'll keep Granny out of the way when it comes,' she promised. 'In fact, I can suggest that she comes into town with me to choose a wreath.'

'That's a good idea!' Jack applauded.

Both his and Harry's face brightened. Mother would not

be put to any unnecessary pain and there would be no need to bring the luggage lift into operation.

Mrs Winthorpe came back into the drawing room.

'I've said goodbye to Nurse,' she said. 'I gave her a handbag from my Christmas store. It wasn't a very good one, but she seemed quite pleased.'

'She was nice, wasn't she, Granny?' Joanna asked. 'I mean, he liked her?'

'Oh, yes, I think so. She was very quiet and didn't talk too much. You know how he dislikes a talker.'

A smile passed round them all. They knew how much he disliked competition!

'Granny,' said Joanna. 'Shall we go into the florist's presently and choose some flowers?'

'Yes,' said Mrs Winthorpe vaguely. She was wondering about that handbag: was it good enough? Then she said more certainly: 'Yes. What time?'

Joanna glanced at Harry.

'Why don't you go at a quarter past three?' he suggested, examining his fingernails. 'Then you'd be back in time for tea.'

'That sounds all right. Will that suit you, Granny?'

'Yes. I'll just slip up and change into black before we go, I think.' Oh dear, she'd have to pass his door again. She had simply rushed past on the way down this morning, holding her breath so as not to smell the stale smoke which still seemed to creep after her from under the door (as though he were still – there). She had taken care not to go upstairs again since. What a pity she hadn't put on all black this morning.

But she'd been in such a fluster she'd thought grey would do, and then found a bit of green had got in by mistake – and that certainly wouldn't do.

The door opened quietly and Brian came in. His face, healthily pink, and usually so pleasant, was unsmiling.

Jack said quickly: 'Hello, old boy! We were sorry we couldn't catch you this morning before you left.' He looked at Brian's red and navy striped tie.

'Yes,' said Brian coldly. 'It was a pity.'

He was extremely angry. Not, as he had said to Elizabeth on the telephone that morning, because he had not been informed: but because they had all gone trooping off to bed, calmly and obliviously sleeping while the Old Man died. And if that was not bad enough, they had actually not even allowed themselves to be disturbed by having the news broken to them that he *had* died. If he had known that was how they were going to behave, he would have stayed himself last night, instead of going home.

He sat down, carefully pulling up the well-creased trousers of his navy pinstripe suit, took the neatly-folded handkerchief out of his breast pocket and brushed it backwards and forwards under his nose. He cleared his throat and waited. He was not going to break the ice. Let them!

'I'm so sorry you had to go all the way into the office and back again,' said Mrs Winthorpe.

'Oh, *that* was nothing!' Scorn poured out of him hot as strong brewed tea out of a teapot. But Mrs Winthorpe, wrapped securely in thoughts for the comfort of her children, went unscalded.

Harry could no longer ignore the accusation in Brian's 'Yes – it was a pity' and the very un-black colours of his tie and handkerchief.

'It's all very well . . .' he began.

'Brian!' Jack put in quickly. It was clear that old Brian was already going to be a bit difficult, without Harry adding to it. 'We thought the funeral should be on Thursday.'

'Funeral?' said Brian, raising his eyebrows. 'Funeral? Surely you mean *cremation*?'

Jack and Harry looked at one another in horror. The accusing tone of voice, the tie, the handkerchief, were all forgotten. . . . Ashes whirled round their heads, blurring their nicely planned funeral arrangements.

'What do you mean?' Harry demanded.

'Surely you knew that Father wished to be cremated?'

'I knew nothing of the sort. There was nothing to that effect in the will. As a matter of fact, I made a special point of asking Mr Trent when I saw him recently. Besides, we've made all the arrangements for the funeral now.'

'Well, I can't help that. When I came over to see Father last night he definitely expressed a wish to be cremated.'

Last night! That meant his dying wish! That could not be ignored.

'And for his ashes to be scattered in the grounds.'

There was a long silence.

Mrs Winthorpe and Harry picked their thumbs, Jack picked his nose. The silk of Brian's handkerchief made a gentle rasping noise as he brushed it beneath his nose, backwards and forwards, forwards and backwards. With a final discreet sniff he bunched it up and returned it to his pocket. It was very unsuitable, he thought crossly. Navy blue with red spots! But how could he have known, this morning . . .?

At last Jack spoke.

'We've made all the arrangements for the funeral on Thursday afternoon!' he said plaintively. 'It took us all morning.'

'Mr Russell already had another appointment that afternoon and he put it off specially,' added Harry. 'And we've sent in the announcement to *The Times* saying the time of the service.'

'That is a pity. Of course, if I'd known sooner I could have saved you all this trouble. However . . . Father definitely told me last night that he wished to be cremated.'

If it was Father's last request, then cremated he must be . . . and scattered. . . .

'Where . . . where did he wish to be scattered?' inquired Mrs Winthorpe.

'He didn't actually specify. But I suggest his ashes should be scattered – that is to say, of course, those which are not buried in the family vault – over the part of the estate he loved best.'

'But I don't know which part of the estate he loved best! And we haven't got a family vault!' Mrs Winthorpe wailed.

'Plot, then! Plot!' said Brian, controlling his exasperation very carefully. Vault sounded so much better than plot. What was the point in splitting hairs? And fancy living with someone for over fifty years without knowing his favourite part of the estate!

'What about the rose garden?' Jack suggested.

'Oh, not the *rose* garden!' Mrs Winthorpe protested.

'I suggest,' said Brian, 'that we scatter the ashes by the old stone shrine halfway up the drive. It's a religious monument, after all. Rather suitable, I think.'

The shrine? That meant they would have to pass him every time they went down or came up the drive. Still, perhaps that was preferable to the rose garden, where one liked to sit. If no one had any better suggestions, the shrine it would have to be. Very well, they concurred, with a sigh.

'I'd better go and ring Russell,' said Harry.

'We could leave the funeral service at the time we'd arranged, couldn't we?' asked Jack. 'And have the cremation afterwards?' He looked at Brian. 'After all, cremations are usually private, and there are sure to be crowds of the Old Boy's friends and the people on the estate and so on who would like to go to some sort of service.'

'I entirely agree,' said Brian. 'You'd have to have a service beforehand or a memorial service afterwards. And I think it best to have the service beforehand. There always seems so much point in having the . . . the coffin actually present. But I think you'll have to have the funeral service in the morning and the cremation in the afternoon so as to leave time to get to the crematorium – the best one is about thirty miles away.'

'I don't know a great deal about cremation,' Jack remarked.

Mrs Winthorpe chimed in: 'Neither do I. But personally, I've always wanted to be cremated myself – I've left a note in my glove drawer saying so. But I'd no idea Father did!'

Brian looked down on them all from the height of his superior knowledge. They really knew very little about Father.

Harry heaved himself out of his chair. No point in delaying. If Brian said that was Father's wish, then it was Father's wish. And it must be carried out. But it is strange, he said to himself as he went off to the telephone, that the Old Boy didn't say so to *me*! And he wished the cremation bombshell had not exploded just as he had been going to explain carefully to Brian his point of view and set his mind finally at rest about not sitting up last night.

VII

Joanna glanced at the clock. 'I think we ought to be going to see about the flowers, Granny.'

'Yes, I suppose we should if we're going to be back in time for any tea.'

'Can I come up with you and get an aspirin after all?'

'Yes, of course.' Thank goodness! Now she wouldn't have to pass his door alone.

When they reached that door they both drew a deep breath and hurried past; neither breathed again until the door of Mrs Winthorpe's room was shut securely behind them.

It was dreadful to be so afraid of the dead. Or not afraid, exactly, but that feeling that he was suddenly going to pop out at them . . . when they both knew very well that he could not.

Neither spoke while Mrs Winthorpe rummaged in her wardrobe for something black. Joanna took two aspirin from

the bottle on the bedside table. Both felt there were things that ought to be said: neither liked to begin.

At last Joanna asked: 'Do you really think he wants to be cremated?'

'Well, if Brian – Uncle Brian – said so . . .' Mrs Winthorpe's worried face appeared through the neck of her black dress, and she began to work her arms down the sleeves. 'Bother!' It was too tight really. She hadn't worn it since her brother James died, six years ago; but it was the only suitable all-black dress she had.

'Let me help you.'

'Thank you.' Doing up the buckle of the belt in the last hole, Mrs Winthorpe went on: 'If Brian said that was what Grandfather asked last night, then he must have wanted to be.'

'Yes, I suppose so.'

'It's a pity we didn't know sooner, before Uncle Jack and Uncle Harry had gone to all that trouble making the arrangements. I mean,' she amended, remembering that Brian couldn't very well have told them any sooner, 'it's a pity he hadn't put it in his will. People usually do, I think. Your Great Uncle James did. But according to Mr Trent, Grandfather hadn't. And of course he never said anything to me. He would never discuss anything like that with me. . . .' She sighed, and said: 'You don't know how lucky you are, having a husband like Tony. Perhaps it sounds wicked, saying that, just now . . . but . . . .'

If only she knew! thought Joanna. If only I could tell her – tell someone – if only my own mother were still alive!

'. . . is this hat all right?' Mrs Winthorpe turned back to the mirror to tilt and settle once more the hat already serenely launched upon her head. 'Did you take an aspirin?' She peered into the mirror at Joanna. Then she looked more carefully. 'You do look pale, darling!'

Joanna immediately turned her face away, and Mrs Winthorpe hid her concern under a brisk: 'Don't let yourself get overtired!'

They hurried out, past his door – holding their breath – and as they went downstairs and neared the drawing room they could hear the voices of the three men raised in discussion.

Jack was saying: 'But it means having two whole days of it!'

'Of what?' Mrs Winthorpe moved forward into the conversation.

'Well, Mother,' Jack started to explain, 'we've altered the arrangements with Mr Russell.'

'He was not very pleased,' Harry put in quietly, adding, still more quietly: 'I'm not surprised.'

'The funeral service is going to be on Wednesday morning at eleven-thirty, followed by a cold luncheon, followed by the cremation in the afternoon at two-thirty.'

'Yes, I see. Well, that's only one day.'

'I know,' Jack waved his hand towards Brian. 'But some of the ashes have to be buried in the family pl . . . er, vault . . . and the rest have to be scattered. That can't be done until Thursday. Apparently we can't even collect them until Thursday morning. They won't be cool . . .'

'It can't be done in under two days,' Harry interrupted quickly, frowning at Jack. What lack of tact!

'Oh, dear,' said Mrs Winthorpe. The four days until Thursday evening seemed to stretch in front of her on and on, as far into the future as the hundreds and thousands of days seemed to stretch into the past behind her. Hundreds and thousands of days of Alfred grumbling, Alfred frowning, Alfred complaining, Alfred . . . Alfred. . . .

'And Mother,' Brian walked over to her. 'I really don't think he should stay in the funeral parlour until Wednesday.'

A flicker of alarm widened her eyes. 'No? Well, where?'

'I think he ought to be brought back here.'

Mrs Winthorpe appealed with a look to her two elder sons. She needed confirmation to steel her to acceptance.

They nodded.

'Where?' she said, bravely.

'Well, *I* think he ought to be here. In the drawing room,' said Brian. 'With lots of flowers.' He looked round the pleasant, light room. It had rather a lot of furniture in it, little tables and things, but they could quite easily be shifted to make room.

'Oh, Brian. Not the drawing room,' Mrs Winthorpe protested. It was *her* room! They would all have to sit in the hall – that dreadful gloomy room smelling of smoke, always of smoke. They'd be talking. About him, perhaps. And there he would be, next door. Within earshot. 'It's so near,' she added.

'So near what?'

'Just . . . so near.'

'Well, if you don't want him in the drawing room, perhaps

52

you can think of a suitable alternative?' Brian said coldly. Poor old man, hustling him off like that. Not even allowed to lie in his own drawing room!

'Well . . . I don't know . . .' Mrs Winthorpe looked helpless, appealed again to Harry and Jack.

Jack said: 'I suggested the conservatory. There are flowers already there and . . .'

Harry interrupted testily: 'And I've already said it's far too warm in there.'

Mrs Winthorpe shivered. She glanced at the window. It was open wide. 'Please shut the window, someone,' she said. 'I can feel a draught, I'm sure I can . . . and it's so bad for my rheumatism. It's all right to have the window open while I'm out of the room,' she added hastily, remembering how, the very minute Alfred disappeared out of the hall on his way upstairs to dress for dinner, she used to dash for the window, open it wide, standing well back to let the fresh clean air blow between the curtains into the room, banishing that dreadful stale smoke which must be got rid of even if it meant more rheumatism for her. And then, presently, he'd come down-stairs again and say accusingly 'You've had that window open!' 'Oh, no, Alfred!' she'd say, innocently, or sometimes, hedging. 'Well, only a tiny bit . . . the fire was smoking.' It was so silly, really, so inconsistent, because he always left his bedroom windows open wide, the draught under his door making the whole of that corridor bitter in winter. . . .

'Why not in his bedroom?' But at this suggestion from Harry, Joanna caught his eye, made a slight movement of her head towards Mrs Winthorpe, and frowned.

Mrs Winthorpe, still engrossed in convincing Alfred that he was not being consistent, and that anyway the hall window had not been open, or only the merest fraction, did not notice.

'What a pity,' said Joanna, 'that the old chapel was burnt down.'

On the piece of vacant ground behind the house, enclosed by a yew hedge, and littered with fallen and blackened blocks of stone, they each erected in their minds the chapel which had once stood there, built by the same Catholic family which had built Otterley Hall and the shrine. The chapel would have done very nicely. It would have been very suitable, just as the shrine was suitable for the scattering of the ashes.

But what was the use of wasting time?

'Well, it *has* been burnt down.' said Harry, tumbling his edifice rather crossly back into a jumble of stones. 'Let's have something constructive.'

'How about the library?' said Joanna.

They looked at her, pondering. That seemed quite a good idea. It was not too near. . . .

'Yes.' Brian decided that it was a good idea. 'All his things are in there. Let him be among them.'

'We ought to move his desk over to the window out of the way,' said Harry.

Brian turned to Joanna. 'Do you remember how he used to beetle off in there to have tea on a tray when Mother had tea parties in the hall?'

'Yes! Or when old Mr Russell brought the parish magazine – always just in time for tea.'

'Or Lady Mountford called. . . .'

'Oh, he could hardly wait to pick up his cup and saucer to get away from her!'

'She played a damned good game of . . .'

'Listen, you two, just let's stick to the point,' Harry broke in. All the same, he was very relieved that Brian seemed to be in a better humour, digression or no digression. 'I take it that we're all agreed that he shall go in the library?'

A gentle murmur of assent ran round the group, followed by a sigh of relief. One more problem settled!

'When will he come back?' enquired Mrs Winthorpe.

'Sometime tomorrow, I expect,' said Harry. 'But we can find out for certain when they come for him.'

'Why does he have to go at all?' asked Joanna.

Harry scowled at her and said: 'There are things to be done.'

Mrs Winthorpe shuddered and Joanna took her arm: 'We really ought to go . . .' she said.

Harry opened the drawing room door. As Joanna followed Mrs Winthorpe out of the room he leaned towards her and whispered: 'Not before a quarter past four!'

Joanna nodded.

Mrs Winthorpe had already seated herself in the car, and Joanna was walking round to the driver's seat, when she saw Harry and Brian inside the front door, beckoning to her. She turned back up the steps.

'I say, Joanna,' Brian said, in a hushed voice. 'Do you think he would mind being shaved?'

'What?' It was only a little bit of a beard, just grey silky fluff, so soft!

'Would he mind being shaved? His beard?'

(I said Oh, Grandfather! You've got a beard! and he said I'm afraid it won't have time to grow. . . .)

'It wasn't very long, was it?'

(. . . and I said yes, of course it will, grow it long like Moses).

'No. It had only been growing for a few days. But the point is, would he mind? Being touched, I mean?'

No more than he'd mind dying alone, being sent away . . . . 'Oh, God!' she exclaimed. 'What does it matter what you do to him now?'

They looked at her in horror, and she said more gently: 'No, no, I'm sure he wouldn't mind.'

'That's all right then!' Harry turned away, relieved. 'I'll tell them.'

Joanna put her hand on Brian's arm.

'Brian,' she said, when Harry had gone. 'Do you think . . . could he possibly have woken up, just before he died, and looked out for someone? And seen . . . nobody?'

Suddenly (perhaps because she had dropped the Uncle) it was as if it were his sister Sylvia speaking. 'No,' he replied. 'I don't think so. After all, he was unconscious. . . .'

'But mightn't he have . . .?'

'*No*, Joanna.'

It was a protest rather than an assurance: a protest for both of them against the vision of an old man looking out in vain into the darkness for one last glimpse of a known face before the darkness finally took him.

VIII

Mrs Winthorpe, poised on the brink of the road, watched the stream of traffic and waited patiently for the red light to interrupt its flow.

At her side, Joanna started to move restlessly. Mrs Winthorpe glanced at her and felt alarmed. Joanna had the look of being about to plunge in among the cars and thread her defiant way to the opposite side.

As long as she doesn't take me with her, she thought. She's young and agile, but when you're over seventy . . . Her thought flickered to Joanna in town saying 'We've just got time, come on, follow me, quick!' and disappearing like a will-o'-the-wisp among the traffic as the lights flashed to green, and she was left with great red buses on either side of her, terrifying in their vastness and threatening to crush her as they roared and sped along the margins of the narrow space which was at once her prison and her refuge.

The lights turned to orange. Mrs Winthorpe reached for Joanna's arm. The lights turned red. A last solitary cyclist trickled past.

'Can we go now?'

'Yes, come on. Quick!' Joanna started forward, but still Mrs Winthorpe hung back.

'Are you sure it's all right?'

'Yes, yes! Of course it's all right.'

They set out for the opposite side.

'What a nice firm arm!' Mrs Winthorpe pinched Joanna's arm. The sadness of old age! It was dreadful how muscles went. Her own arm was quite flabby now, yet forty years ago her own grandmother used to say to her what she had just said to her granddaughter.

Suddenly she pinched Joanna's arm harder. 'There's Miss March!' she exclaimed. 'Look – coming down the street. Quick. Let's get into the flower shop before she sees us. She's such a talker.'

'It's no good, she's seen us. She's hurrying.'

Miss March bore down upon them. The light framework of her body seemed at all seasons to be blown before a wind, with draperies fluttering and setting free emanations of winter clothing put away with mothballs, or summer clothing laid by in lavender.

'Oh, Mrs Winthorpe, I'm so sorry to hear your sad news!' She was breathless, almost speechless, with the gust of her arrival. 'The baker told me this morning. It must have been a great shock! I am so, so sorry. . . .'

She clenched her thin fingers against her flat chest, then extended them, offering heartfelt sympathy. She caught Mrs Winthorpe's hand.

'If there's anything I can do to help. . . .' She remembered Joanna, and said: 'Hello, my dear! It's a long time since I've seen you.'

Not since I was so high – tea, chocolate cake and help-snip-the-dead-heads-off-her-roses – ran through Joanna's mind as she greeted Miss March.

'If there's anything I can do to help. . . .' repeated Miss March, urging her bountiful sympathy across the gap between Mary Winthorpe's wealth and position in county society and

her own frugal and parochial existence. Now they were as sisters, sisters in sorrow. The bony fingers increased their pressure.

'Oh, thank you so much. That's very kind of you, but I really don't think . . .' Mrs Winthorpe extricated herself.

'Of course we all knew the Colonel had been ill, but I'd no idea he was *so* ill. It must have been a great shock.'

'Well, yes, of course, it . . .'

'And you had all your family around you, I hope? The little granddaughter I see. . . .'

Joanna endured the brief pat on her shoulder, light as a falling leaf. There was about Miss March something that not only repelled but horrified. Miss March still had the beauty which in the past was, so they said, well known: but now it was surrounded with an aura of mustiness. It was like coming across material, unused and carefully hoarded, which had preserved its beauty throughout the years, showing its age only on careful scrutiny, in its fading, its faint creases and discolourations; yet one knew that throughout the years it had been slowly, surely, deteriorating to the point of decay. At a touch, perhaps, it would fall to pieces.

'Yes, and Harry was home of course. And Jack and Laurine came the day before yesterday,' said Mrs Winthorpe. 'And Brian lives so nice and near.'

'You are very fortunate to have your family around you at a time like this!' Miss March, alone in the world, smiled sadly. She turned to Joanna:

'And how's that charming husband of yours I've heard so much about?'

'Quite well, thank you.'

'Is he with you, too?'

'No. I – I just came over for the afternoon. I shall be going back this evening.' She couldn't even say the word 'home' now. There was no home for her where Tony was. Home was just a house now.

'Miss March, we mustn't stop. We really mustn't!' Mrs Winthorpe started to draw away from what she knew would develop into an inquisition first of Joanna, later of herself. 'We have so much to do and we must get on to the florist's to order the flowers for Wednesday.'

Miss March fluttered after her. 'The flowers! Oh, could I do the flowers for the church? As you say, you have so much to do and I would love to do something for the Colonel in return for all he's done for me!'

For many years he had sent her from his farm frequent gifts of butter and eggs – less frequent during and just after the war, of course – and each Christmas a fat goose. He was the kindest man she had ever known. *She* would be proud to be the widow of such a man!

Mrs Winthorpe felt Miss March follow her into the shop, as tenacious as a piece of dead stick caught up in her skirt.

While her grandmother and Miss March discussed together the flowers for the church, Joanna made her way to a great bowl of roses in a corner of the shop and, bending over them, she breathed in their sweet, rich scent. Home! she thought. Just a house! She remembered how she had come into that house two years ago, filled with excitement at being grown up, free at last, mistress in a home of her very own.

She had tried so hard to make it a home that a man could be proud of, choosing colours and materials which she thought Tony would like. But somehow, something had always been wrong. Either they were too bright, or too dark, or too rough, or too smooth. Or too expensive. Quite often they were too expensive.

At first, Tony pointed out her mistakes with a rueful smile and a little joke such as, 'Never mind, sweet, after the way you've been brought up we mustn't expect miracles, must we?' – a brave little joke, made as if to cover up the disappointment which he nevertheless allowed to show in his face.

Later, as she tried to run the house that she had been unable to decorate or furnish to his satisfaction, he found more and more cause for complaint. There were bones in his fish, stones in his cherries, his trousers were not properly pressed, his gravy was not made as mother used to make it, why must she go to the cinema twice in one week, why should she use the car, why was she always gadding about anyway, wasn't she content with her own home? The little jokes became less frequent, and the pale, rather prominent eyes projected resentment in place of disappointment.

For two years she tried to be what Tony wanted, listened to his complaints, tried to do better, failed, tried again, failed . . . round and round like a squirrel in a cage, day after day. And at night in bed she cried, after he had finished with her body and she was alone again.

Then came Andrew, loving her and believing in her. Andrew made her feel a woman, where Tony had made her feel less than an animal. Strength began to return to her. She

began to listen to a new small voice inside her which said: you are a human being with a will of your own; only you have the right to direct that will. A core of rebellion began to form inside her. Tony's resentment turned into suspicion and a smouldering rage that would have terrified her less had it erupted into violence instead of lying just concealed beneath the smooth but ever-increasing flow of gentle-voiced complaints in private and public performances of love and tenderness. She struggled against him, but she had not been able to regain enough strength in time – the strength to go with Andrew.

Andrew came into her heart again, and the pain began to radiate outwards through her body. It was cut short mercifully by her grandmother.

'Joanna!'

She lifted her head.

'What are you thinking about, child? I've asked you twice if you think Madonna lilies and yellow roses would be nice for the church.'

'Oh, I'm sorry, Granny!' She looked away from Miss March's inquisitive gaze. 'Yes – yes, I'm sure they'd be lovely.'

'That's all right, then. So does Miss March.' The order was given for a sufficient but not ostentatious quantity of flowers to be delivered at the church on Wednesday morning.

Now, thought Mrs Winthorpe, I hope Miss March will go and leave us to choose our personal wreaths and crosses by ourselves. Perhaps, after all, I'll have a wreath. Alfred was not really a religious man . . . 'Oh, goodbye, Miss March! Must you really go? Well . . . thank you so very much. . . .'

Miss March left with a last bony pressure (so painful for rheumatism) of Mrs Winthorpe's hand and a flutter of fingers at Joanna. They watched her through the glass window, over the heads of the flowers, going down the street rather slowly, her silk scarf floating endlessly out behind her as she wove in and out among the people crowding the pavement, making her unsteady drifting way – where?

'Now Joanna . . .' What a relief. But hush. She was very kind. 'What shall I get? I don't really know . . . do you think a cross? Or a wreath? Or a lyre?'

'Grandfather was not very musical, so why a lyre?'

'No. But then he wasn't religious, either. Do you think a wreath?'

'Yes, that seems more non-committal. What of?'

'Roses are lovely.'

'You're having them for the church.'

'I could have a different colour for the wreath. Not pink. He didn't care for pink. Those dark crimson ones are lovely.'

'Yes, they are indeed.' But, Joanna wondered sadly, would her grandmother ever realise the irony of those red roses – red roses for love?

'Yes, I think I'll have them,' Mrs Winthorpe decided. 'What are you going to have? The sweet peas are beautiful.'

Joanna looked at them – frivolous dancing butterflies. Quite unsuitable.

Suddenly she saw the irises, great deep bronze flags with purple falls. 'I'll have those. In a sheaf.'

Mrs Winthorpe looked and approved. 'That's settled then. They can all be sent together tomorrow afternoon when the

others have chosen theirs. You're going to have the irises, and I shall have a wreath of roses.'

The words of an old tune, 'She Wore a Wreath of Roses,' were sung in Mrs Winthorpe's memory by a tall man leaning over the piano on which she was accompanying him. She couldn't remember the time or the place or even the man – just the song – and the words floated ridiculously in and out of the order she was giving to that nice girl in green.

IX

As Joanna drove Mrs Winthorpe away in the car to choose the flowers, Brian followed Harry back into the drawing room.

Jack was stretching himself, anchored by one arm to Laurine; he looked down at her through half-closed eyelids as he yawned.

'Come along,' he groaned, on the dying note of his yawn. 'We must go for a walk. Get a breath of fresh air.'

Like a young sparrow in her new grey dress, Laurine chirped assent demurely from beneath his arm. She perched herself on the edge of the sofa, ready to go.

They moved off, side by side.

'I've a good mind to go and have a sleep,' Harry announced.

'Not now! Surely you don't need to sleep *now*?' Brian protested.

Harry looked at his watch. 'Twenty-five past three,' he grumbled. 'I suppose it's hardly worth it. Wrightson's will be here any minute. But I do dislike missing my afternoon sleep.'

'Today's a little different, don't you think? After all, there are, to put it mildly, one or two things to discuss.' Brian sat down on the sofa and spread his hands on his knees.

'I think most things have been taken care of quite adequately.'

'Well, there's one thing I can think of straight away which hasn't . . .'

'Oh? What's that?'

'Have you realised how little time there is to get back here from the church after the service in the morning, and then on to the crematorium afterwards? It's about an hour's drive, you know, allowing for traffic . . . it will leave very little time for lunch.'

'Well, people will hardly expect to sit down to a whacking great feast, will they?'

'No, not a *feast*. But all the same you can hardly hustle people from pillar to post like that, can you? It's scarcely dignified at a funeral, is it?'

'There is no question of hustling people from pillar to post. We shall have at least three-quarters of an hour for lunch. That's long enough for anyone.'

'Of course it is – if you're going to travel the whole way to the crematorium – hearse and all – at eighty miles an hour!'

Harry sighed, to let Brian know that he was *trying* to be patient. Then he lowered himself on the sofa beside his brother. He might as well be comfortable too.

'There will not be the slightest necessity to go at eighty,' he said. 'The whole thing has been most carefully timed.'

Brian got up and went to the window. He stood, with his back to Harry, looking out.

The funeral procession rattled past at eighty miles an hour.

It was quite fantastic! Of *course* there was not enough time!

He swung round suddenly to face Harry: 'What about the funeral cars?'

'Wrightson's are arranging all that.'

'But where are they getting the cars from?'

'Local hire, I suppose.'

'But do you mean to say . . .? Good heavens! This is quite incredible!' Brian walked back to where Harry was still sitting, and stood looking down on him while slowly turning over the contents of his trouser pockets. 'Do you mean to say you were actually planning to have *local taxis* in the procession?'

'I don't see why not.'

'But . . . my dear Harry!' Brian ran the tip of his tongue over his lips; then he bent over Harry kindly, solicitously. He felt infinitely older and wiser than his elder brother. If Harry didn't know how things should be done then he must be helped, guided. 'Surely you must see that's quite impossible?'

'Why?'

'Why? Well . . . don't you realise . . .' Brian paused and straightened himself slowly, giving Harry plenty of time to get ready to realise: then he bent forward again and said: 'Don't you realise that the Old Man was a figure in the county?'

The Colonel stood before them: a monumental figure, towering over the Derbyshire peaks.

Harry was silent. Barging in, he was saying to himself,

upsetting arrangements, scattering cars and ashes all over the place. . . .

'OBE and JP' Brian reminded him, very gently.

'Then,' Harry said at last, 'what do you suggest? A fleet of Rolls-Royces?'

'Yes. Or, at the very least, Daimlers. If I had known before I left for the office this morning I could have laid the whole thing on for you from there. . . .'

'You'd better lay it on now!' said Harry shortly.

'Well, I'll certainly try. But it'll be a little difficult now. It's been left rather late, you see. However . . . mind you, I can't make any promises but I'll do my best. Naturally. How many cars were ordered?'

'Three. Mother and Jack will go in our own Rolls.'

It would be the first time in her life, thought Brian, that she would not have to ask the Old Man for permission to use the car.

'And,' Harry went on, 'you and I and Elizabeth and Laurine will go in the first of the hired cars, Joanna and Tony in the second, and that'll leave a spare one in case anyone wants a lift back from the church.'

'Good,' said Brian. 'Then that's settled. I'll see to it first thing tomorrow morning.' He looked at Harry sharply. 'How do you think Joanna's looking?'

'Joanna! What on earth has she got to do with the funeral cars?'

'Nothing. It was just that your mentioning her name reminded me. . . . I thought she seemed very nervous today, very much on edge.'

'You mean . . .?'

'I mean,' said Brian, 'have you had any more conversations with Tony about this – this nonsense about Joanna and some other man? Andrew, I think you said his name was?'

Harry rubbed his chin thoughtfully. 'Actually,' he said, 'I haven't. Not since Tony came down and saw me that day I told you about a few weeks ago.'

'What I don't quite understand . . .' said Brian slowly, watching Tony in his mind talking earnestly to Harry, gentle, hurt, but wanting only the best for everyone, '. . . is why he came to you? After all, surely a thing like that is between him and Joanna?'

'I can understand perfectly well why he came to me. He told me why. He needed someone to turn to for advice. As you know, he's never made any secret of the fact that he has no relatives whatsoever in this country – after all, he is an Australian by birth even if his family was originally English. I'm very sorry for the poor chap. Joanna's always been a handful, too!'

Harry recalled some of the pranks Joanna used to get up to as a child. Making apple pie beds, putting hairbrushes and whoopee cushions in awkward places, even tying his entire room up with string once. String stretched all over the bed like a pig net so he couldn't get into it; string from the lamps to the curtain rods, from the door handle to the handles of the wardrobe and chest of drawers, balls and balls of it. It had taken him two hours to undo it all and roll it up into balls again. He had given her a good lecture afterwards, but it didn't seem to have much effect because shortly afterwards

there had been the episode of the Eno's in his jerry. He hated to think of that. He blamed Mother for a lot of it, of course. She was far too indulgent with Joanna. Father had treated her much more sensibly. Father had been the only person who made any impression on her.

He visualised her now not as a mature, full-breasted, beautiful woman, but as the rather plain, mischievous, laughing child still in need of kindly discipline. He hoped Tony was firm enough with her.

'Yes,' he repeated, 'she's always been a handful. And so was her mother,' he added.

'Sylvia was a sweetie!' Brian retorted.

'I'm not saying she wasn't. I was just as fond of her as you were. She was my sister too, remember. And I'm fond of Joanna – don't think I'm not – but she's got a good husband in Tony and I'm going to do what I can to see that she doesn't forget it. It's very decent of Tony to give her another chance, in the circumstances.'

'I suppose so.'

'And a divorce in the family would be unthinkable. We've never had such a thing before.'

'There's got to be a first time for everything. And I, personally, think some marriages are better brought to an end rather than having two people living in misery for the rest of their lives.' He thanked goodness *he* could not be counted in such a category, and congratulated himself on having chosen a wife like Elizabeth – sweet-tempered, kind, intelligent, and immensely pretty into the bargain. The trouble with people who married too young was that they were simply incapable

of weighing things up properly. He had waited, sensibly, until he was over thirty. He had got his reward. 'Look at Sylvia,' he continued. 'What sort of a life do you think she would have had if she'd lived?'

'That was different. Dennis was an absolute rotter. We all knew that. I think under those circumstances even divorce would be . . . but you cannot possibly compare that marriage with Joanna's.'

'You usually find there's fault on both sides when a marriage goes wrong. If there's any truth in this story of Tony's. . . .'

'If there's any truth? You surely don't imagine Tony would lie?'

'You are convinced then? You trust him?'

'Oh, implicitly. You have only to look at him. He's as straight as a die.'

'Well, I hope so. I certainly hope so. And I hope he is as good a husband as you appear to think and that Joanna doesn't forget it. I hope everyone will live happily ever after. As you say, we certainly don't want a family scandal. . . .'

'We're not going to have one,' said Harry firmly. 'And really, you know, this is scarcely the time to be talking about such things!'

They sat silent for a few minutes while they directed their thoughts decorously along the funeral route.

'Morning coats and top hats, of course,' Brian said suddenly. He wouldn't put it past Harry to want to go in a lounge suit!

Harry decided it would be better not to mention that he had been pondering over going in a lounge suit (dark one, of

course), 'Yes, naturally,' he said. He hoped it would not be too hot on Wednesday. 'I can hardly get into my morning coat.'

'I can't get into mine at all. I had to hire one for the last wedding I went to.'

'Well, of course, you prosperous businessmen!' A smile started to broaden across Harry's face. 'What do you expect when you spend about three hours at lunch every day and never do a stroke of work?'

'What nonsense! Why, sometimes I only have half an hour, sometimes only a sandwich . . .'

'Ah, sometimes, maybe!'

'. . . and as for work, I have to get up at half past six every morning to catch the 7.55 – *as you know –* '

In the distance Laurine's high chatter sounded.

'Seen the will yet?' asked Brian quickly.

'No. I think the proper time to read that is after the funeral. I've telephoned Mr Trent and asked him to have three copies done, for you, myself and Jack. We shall have them by Thursday. I did think you and I might have gone down to see Mr Trent this afternoon, but there obviously wasn't going to be much time.'

'I couldn't get here much more quickly than I did, all things being considered.'

Jack and Laurine came in.

'Wrightson's are here,' said Jack. 'We saw them coming up the drive as we came in.'

'I'll go and have a word with them.' Harry got up and made for the door.

Jack looked after him doubtfully. Hang it, he ought to have stayed and seen to that himself.

Laurine walked over to Brian and standing close in front of him she said: 'How is Elizabeth?'

'Fine, thanks.' He edged backwards slightly and, as she still remained standing in front of him, searched in the succeeding silence for something to talk about. His search was impeded by Harry's voice, sounding now loud, now soft, like a radio with uncontrolled volume, directing the undertaker's men. 'This way . . . stairs . . . third left . . . change in plans . . . tonight . . . morning . . . you think . . .' All words became indistinguishable. Harry's voice died away, the tramp of feet moved on up the stairs and passed overhead.

'How is Simon? Dear little boy. You are lucky to have such a nice little boy.' She lowered her eyelids and shot a glance at Jack, appealingly, she hoped, seductively . . . She was disappointed and slightly irritated to find it wasted, for Jack was gazing out of the window with his back to her.

She looked up at Brian again (but demurely – butter mustn't melt in her mouth!) and said fervently, hoping that this time Jack would overhear: 'I *do* envy you.'

Oh, my God! Brian said to himself. Surely not at Jack's age. . . .

Jack gave a sudden loud snort, startling Brian and Laurine – he must have been listening all the time. '*I* don't envy Brian!' he said. 'Thank you very much. *I* don't want squalling brats and nappies and things all over the place at my time of life.'

'Oh, darling!' Laurine ran over to take his arm and rub her cheek against his sleeve.

Oh, God! thought Brian.

Footsteps sounded in the corridor above, with the slow, steady rhythmical tread of men who bore a heavy burden.

'Go on!' said Jack, laughing. 'Temptress! Get thee behind me!' He gave Laurine a playful slap. He followed that up with a pinch. Really, she had a very nice bottom!

Her playful protest burst like shattered glass into Brian's silent count of one-two, one-two, in time with those footsteps which were passing overhead along the passage to the stairs, growing louder, nearer, descending.

'Steady!' said a voice.

Laurine stopped her provocative retreat: the smile left her face. Jack, too, had heard: with his hand still outstretched towards Laurine he stood, listening.

'Easy round the corner!'

The footsteps descended the last flight of stairs; they passed by the drawing room door, still in perfect time; the front door creaked heavily open; then shut.

A few moments later a motor started up, moved off and faded into the distance.

Gone!

Harry opened the drawing room door into silence.

THE SECOND DAY

I

Laurine yawned and stretched, slowly savouring with familiar delight the utmost giving of each muscle and its return to flexible ease. She lay in bed, warm and relaxed, for there was still time to idle, to let her mind wander here and there: through the open window into the promise of another perfect summer day; to the garden; to the swimming pool, where later she would go for a swim, alone because nothing would induce Jack or Harry to bathe. Tony would, if he'd been coming in the daytime instead of after the office – Joanna, too. When Tony looked at you in a swimsuit, it made you feel quite something.

She glanced at Jack, asleep beside her with his mouth slightly open. If he had been twenty years younger would he have come swimming with her? It seemed such a waste of that lovely pool, surrounded with high copper beech hedges so that one could bathe without a stitch on and afterwards lie naked in the sun.

Why did a man change after marriage? A year ago Jack used to take her out dancing almost every night, give her presents – chocolates, fruit, flowers – but after they were married, although he was, of course, just as sweet and kind and attentive, he never seemed to want to go out dancing. He was getting too old, he said. Not that she regretted for one minute . . . even though she had given up such a promising stage career . . . she might have been a star now . . .

She sighed. Perhaps now (since yesterday morning – only twenty-four hours ago although it seemed years) they would be able to have some fun again. Perhaps they could get a bigger house and a car and servants, dancing, theatres, holidays abroad. Jack would be able to afford all those things now, and she could surely persuade him at least to temporary youth.

If only they could have a baby! How could a man have a baby and not feel young himself?

She put her arm across him and pressed her body close against his: 'Wake up, darling!' She nuzzled his neck, kissing gently, quickly.

He gave a grunt. 'Oh, Lord! It's not time to get up yet, is it?'

'No, of course not, darling. I haven't even poured out your tea.'

'Thank God.' He burrowed down again. 'I loathe getting up in the morning. Especially when I've got you to lie in bed with!'

She laughed happily. That, at any rate, was one way in which he remained young. He was just as eager as a young man. Almost too eager at times. Still, she wasn't going to complain. One never knew how long that could be kept up, so she was going to make hay while the sun shone.

Unbuttoning his pyjama jacket and slipping her hand over his bare chest, she said: 'Jack!', paused to look into his face, and then rubbed her cheek against his beard. Nice it smelt. Eau de Cologne. 'Did you really mean you didn't want a baby when you said that yesterday afternoon about nappies and things?'

'Of course I did. I'm much too old to start a family now.'

'But, darling, you're not old. You're young.'

'I must say, I *feel* young enough – with you.'

'And a baby would be lovely, and you'd love it, I know you would. And I wouldn't let it cry where it could disturb you when you were painting, or put nappies and things where you could see them. Honestly, you'd never know it was in the house.'

'What's the point of having it, then?'

'Oh!' She gave an exasperated wriggle away from him. 'You know what I mean. Up till now, you've always said we couldn't afford a baby. But couldn't we? Now?'

She moved closer to him again, lifting her head to look at him imploringly.

'Well, any extra money we have' – and he hoped to God there *was* going to be some – 'can quite easily be disposed of without going to all the trouble of having a baby. We can have a servant . . .'

'I don't want a servant! I don't mind a bit going on doing all the cooking and housework if I can have a baby. And I'd look after the baby too.'

'Oh, you're wonderful, darling! You're beautiful, and I adore you!' He slipped her nightgown off her shoulder in order to kiss the warm, naked flesh. It was firm and rounded and downy: he wanted to bite it. 'When I'm a rich man' – or comparatively – 'I'll give you anything you want' – or almost – 'but you're not going to talk me into giving you a baby!'

She wrenched herself free from his eagerly travelling lips and, jerking her nightdress into place, sprang out of bed.

'Hey! Where are you off to?' Jack exclaimed, surprised and frustrated by the suddenness of her departure.

'I'm going to get dressed. I'm going out for a walk. I'm not going to waste time lying in bed on a lovely morning like this.'

'But you always like lying in bed in the mornings. Besides, it's only a quarter past eight. And you haven't poured my tea.'

'Pour it yourself!' She gathered up her clothes and flounced off to the bathroom. She knew it gave him pleasure to watch her dress. This morning he wasn't going to get even that.

'Little bitch!' Jack exclaimed, half-exasperated, half-laughing; and folding his arms behind his head he resigned himself to the waste of half an hour in bed alone. She'd come round presently; perhaps soon. He glanced at the clock, hoping.

She was such a delectable little piece. And usually so willing. My God, she was good.

He twisted uncomfortably in the bed. He'd better think about something else. What was the good of torturing oneself?

Supposing he really did have no more money coming to him, as the Old Boy had threatened. What would happen to Laurine when he died? He was over fifty, Laurine twenty-five. One had to make some sort of provision – a regular job? Oh,

God, fancy getting up every morning to catch the 7.55! Ghastly!

Old Brian might do that sort of thing, but then Brian was cut out for it. He and Harry had always been the efficient ones, romping through exams at Harrow, graduating from Oxford, while he – well, he got by somehow, though not at all to Father's satisfaction (although he'd excelled at cricket, which was more than Harry or Brian had. *They'd* never played in the First Eleven!). Father's comments when he failed his law exams had been hot and acrid as a shower of cayenne pepper falling round his head, bowed guiltily as he remembered long summer days spent sketching by the river instead of swotting. A worse storm followed when he announced that he was going to become an artist, which Father somehow associated with the word 'penniless'. He had nevertheless managed, with a hoist or two from one-man exhibitions financed by Mother, to make for himself a moderately successful career and earn a modest income which would in due course be supplemented considerably.

For nearly thirty years he had painted contentedly, untroubled by women, or at least not troubled to the extent of wishing to marry one. Then, just over a year ago, he had taken on the designing of the stage set for *No Bells for Miss Martin*, in which there was a promising young actress named Laurine May. She had troubled him a lot. So much, in fact, that, completely bowled over, there had been only one thing to do – to marry her. He did it. And told the family afterwards.

He had expected a rumpus, of course, but not quite such a devil of a rumpus. Father had been young once, must

have been, so he ought to have understood how one felt. Nevertheless, purple in the face, moustache bristling, he had raked up all the old stuff about not getting into the Sixth at Harrow (the First Eleven forgotten, of course), failing his Finals at Oxford, wasting all the money spent on giving him a decent education, leading a bohemian life, the word penniless even cropped up now and again, finally ending in the explosive threat: 'You'll neither of you get a penny when my time comes.'

Old Harry had interceded with Father. Old Harry always did his best. But it had no visible effect. Father's last words on the subject had been said and one simply did not know whether or not he had in fact carried out his threat. The only ray of hope was that he had always treated Laurine with courtesy and kindness once she became his daughter-in-law.

Jack heard the bathroom door open. Laurine's quick, light steps pattered along the passage towards the bedroom. She'd be in in a moment to say she was sorry, to kiss him. Little tease. He raised his head to listen better and began to hope eagerly (it was only half past eight – breakfast wasn't until nine). But her footsteps passed the door and went on down the stairs.

He fell back on his pillow, disappointed, but still half-amused. She'd come running presently to kiss and make up. At breakfast probably. But that would be too late. This was a bloody waste of time.

He kicked off the covers and swung his legs over the side of the bed. He caught a glimpse of himself in the long mirror as he tugged undone the string of his pyjama trousers and let them fall to the ground. He slipped out of the jacket, already unbuttoned by Laurine, and stood looking at himself with his chest thrown out and his stomach tucked in. He thanked God that he didn't have a bow window in front like Harry and Brian. *He* had kept his figure although he was older than them. Not bad for a man of fifty. Not bad at all.

II

Upjohn was putting the dish of sausages on the electric heater to keep warm (the family were rarely down punctually for breakfast, even Mr Harry) when the dining room door opened and to her surprise in strolled Mr Jack, spick and span, on a wave of Eau de Cologne. Upjohn frowned. She disapproved of scent for men. Mr Harry would never use it.

She replied rather stiffly to Mr Jack's greeting. She hadn't brought in the coffee or the hot milk; hadn't rung the gong, nor propped open the dining room door for admittance.

She stalked out to fetch the coffee and milk. When she came back into the dining room he said: 'Hasn't Mrs Jack come in yet?'

Upjohn's surprise increased. Neither of them got up early as a rule (canoodling in bed until the last possible moment).

'No, Sir. I haven't seen her since I brought up your early tea.'

'It was such a nice day, she thought she'd like a walk before breakfast.' Be breezy! One doesn't want the servants to think there's anything up. 'I expect she'll be in any moment now.'

Jack clapped his hands and rubbed them together with a brisk cheerfulness he was not feeling.

'I haven't rung the gong yet, Sir,' Upjohn reproved. 'I was just about to.'

'Good!' Quite unabashed, he walked over to the sideboard, lifted the lid off the sausages and smelled them.

Mr Harry would never have done a thing like that! Upjohn propped open the door and went to ring the gong. There was Mrs Jack just coming in the front door. She gave Upjohn a quick, almost apologetic smile as she hurried past her into the dining room.

Upjohn paused for a moment before ringing the gong. She hoped to goodness there hadn't been a tiff. Of course it was no business of hers, but . . .

Then she heard: 'Hello, darling!' and 'Hello, darling!' and the sound of a kiss, two kisses, three. . . . She dealt the gong a rain of mighty blows.

The thought suddenly struck her: fit to awaken the dead!

But he wasn't even in the house. Be back after lunch, though.

It would be queer to have his coffin standing in the library, where she'd so often taken his tea when there were visitors he didn't want to see. They'd cleared a good space in the middle of the room. The trestles were in place. Everything was ready for him.

I must go and see about collecting some more money for a wreath, she told herself, going into the pantry and picking up a piece of paper and a pencil to make out a list.

Everyone would subscribe, of course. Some willingly, some

grudgingly; some generously, some meanly. But no one would refuse . . . out of respect, out of liking, out of not wanting the others to know they had refused. The names would appear on the card with the wreath.

Mrs Burton had already given half-a-crown, anticipating Upjohn's request, and young Jim had offered a shilling when he brought up the morning milk from the farm.

Upjohn decided to go round on her bicycle for the rest of the collecting after she'd cleared in the dining room. She'd have to look sharp, because Mr Harry had kindly offered her a lift when he took Mr and Mrs Jack down with him to choose their wreaths. Mr Harry was so good about lifts.

Ah, she said to herself, hearing the back door open and familiar boots tread along the stone passage. That's Brown with the fruit and vegetables. That'll save a visit to the garden, at any rate. He'll know to bring his offering in. He knows what's what.

She heard the thud of the vegetable basket on the kitchen table. Then Brown himself came along the passage to the pantry and, with a gruff 'Good morning' deposited a basket of strawberries on the scrubbed wooden table.

'Good morning, Mr Brown.' Upjohn took the basket and emptied the strawberries into a clean dish. 'It's a nice day again.'

'Not much good bringing in the raspberries,' said Brown. 'No one seems to eat 'em except the Colonel. And he won't be eating any more.'

'I expect he's happy enough where he is.' She handed back the empty basket, paused for a moment to see the Colonel

comfortable among the clouds, then went on: 'Mr Harry asked me to say that if anyone wants to come this afternoon and see the coffin and the flowers, it'll be in the library at three o'clock. I'm sure you'll want to subscribe towards the wreath, Mr Brown?'

'Of course.' He was only sorry that he had not been able to make a wreath of flowers from his garden, but the flower garden was not what it used to be, thanks to the war. Times had changed.

He held out a pound note. 'This is from me and the Missus and Tommy.'

'Oh, thanks, Mr Brown!' Upjohn was delighted to feel the crisp note in her hand. That would swell the collection. They'd end up with a lovely wreath at this rate. 'That is good of you.'

'He was always good to me.' Brown hitched the empty basket on his arm and trudged out of the pantry.

Upjohn followed him to the door and watched his rather bent back receding along the passage. How he had aged lately. Morning after morning, for over forty years, she'd seen him and he'd scarcely seemed to alter. And now, all of a sudden, his hair seemed to have whitened; his back to have bent; his walk to have become slow and laboured.

She went to look in the cracked mirror which hung over the pantry sink. It had hung there ever since she first came as under-parlourmaid. Drat! Those grey hairs were beginning to show again. She must give them another touch up or she'd be looking more than her sixty years!

She collected Mrs Winthorpe's breakfast tray from upstairs. Then she went into the serving room to see how they were

getting on in the dining room. There was a lot to do today: four for lunch, eight for dinner.

Mr Harry was down, of course, and she could hear Mr Jack's voice saying something about Mr Trent . . . the will . . .

She moved away from the door. She didn't approve of listeners. Besides, there was quite a gap under that door and they could probably see her feet.

They did take a time over breakfast! Pity Mrs Winthorpe didn't see fit to get up for it these days. She might have got them moving – although even in the old days, when the Colonel had shooting parties for going out after grouse on the moors, they used sometimes to sit over breakfast until gone ten o'clock, while he told stories. How could one be expected to clear, wash up and lay for lunch (maybe for twenty or more) on time?

She returned to her list. Taking a stump of pencil from behind the blue tea caddy on the shelf she put a tick beside Mrs Burton, Brown and family and Jim Bobbett.

Then she went through to the front of the house in search of Mrs Bannister.

It was a nuisance having no living-in housemaid. These dailies never came until nine. They'd only just get done in the hall and drawing room before the family had finished breakfast, and then there they'd be messing about in the dining room half the morning instead of the downstairs being all done before breakfast as it was in the old days. Good gracious, the housemaids (four of them) would have been down by six o'clock, sweeping, dusting, polishing, so that all looked as neat as a new pin by the time the family came down.

Upjohn sighed for the good old days. Wages had been less – sixteen pounds a year was all she'd had to start. But money went further in those days and she'd had plenty of good plain food, enough clothes. . . . And there'd been an under-chauffeur once, a long time ago, Charles (a handsome lad!) – but that had never come to anything. A kiss under the mistletoe one Christmas; walking out on alternate Sundays for a month or two; then along came Polly the nurserymaid, flighty young piece. That had been that.

'Don't forget the library whatever you do,' Upjohn warned Mrs Bannister, after coaxing half-a-crown (only one hour's wage!) out of her.

She returned to the pantry and as soon as she heard the dining room door open she bustled through to pounce on the breakfast things. She washed up quickly. They'd have to dry on the draining-board just for this once. Sometimes when there were extra in the house Mr Harry would give her a hand with the drying – a lovely job he made of it too, polishing the glasses and all – but of course he was much too busy today.

She wiped her hands, took off her apron and replaced her cap with a large mauve straw hat, and bustled out to the bicycle shed.

III

Mrs Winthorpe, on her way downstairs, looked out of the landing window and saw Upjohn perched very upright on her high, old-fashioned bicycle. It was that same old thing she had when she first came to Otterley as a girl. It was as much a part of her as the mauve hat skewered to the still ungreyed bun (was it dyed or what?), the afternoon caps with muslin streamers (where did she buy such things these days?) and the big purple umbrella she always carried on wet days off.

Mrs Winthorpe watched Upjohn, dignified and disdainful, sailing over the gravel, with her head held high and looking straight ahead of her. Going to collect for the wreath, supposed Mrs Winthorpe, and remembered unhappily that he was coming back today. She wasn't quite sure what time they were bringing him: there'd been so many arrangements made and altered, and everything was somehow rather a muddle. She really didn't know where she was half the time, felt all at sea and just had to let it wash around her. Someone would hold her head above water. . . .

Nevertheless she would have to arrange about food for tonight. All the family would be here for dinner: Brian, Elizabeth, Tony, Joanna, all arriving this afternoon sometime. And Wednesday (tomorrow) – how many would there be for lunch tomorrow? It would depend on who came to the funeral, of course, but she hoped they wouldn't ask a great many back – it was really only necessary to ask relatives and *very* close friends. And not a great big meal. That wouldn't be at all necessary. Something light and cold. She'd speak to Mrs Burton as soon as she got downstairs, go straight to the kitchen. Catering was dreadfully difficult nowadays.

She was sick of housekeeping. Fifty-three years of it, oh *much* too long.

Upjohn's erect back sailed down the drive past the grey stone shrine on the corner.

That was where the ashes were going to be scattered.

Mrs Winthorpe was suddenly appalled that soon ashes would be all that would be left.

She turned away from the window and went quickly on down the stairs.

Upjohn sighed with relief as she got past the shrine. She never cared for it much. Queer old thing, that it was. Why did they leave a thing like that up when they weren't Catholics? Quite frightening it was in the moonlight, as though it had something hidden in it which might leap out and grab her as she came back from her half-day. But it didn't frighten *her*, she told herself, now she was past it.

She turned off the drive and went down the farm road. It badly needed mending. She bounced up and down as the bicycle wheels bumped over ruts and puddle holes. Thank goodness her hat was pinned on securely! The brakes rattled and the loose bit of celluloid on the handle scratched her right palm; the bell jingled a tune to every bump. It was almost falling to pieces, the old boneshaker, but she wouldn't part with it for worlds.

She met the bailiff coming out of the farmyard, passed the time of day with him briefly (she never did like that man!), came straight to the point of the wreath and increased her fund by a further ten shillings.

She couldn't be sure, of course, but it struck her that the note was passed a little unwillingly; more as if for the show of the thing than from the fullness of Mr Lipton's heart. Nor had he seemed honoured, nor even particularly interested, when she informed him that if he wished to pay his last respects he

might do so this afternoon when the coffin would be on view in the library at three o'clock.

She felt that he bore a grudge, somehow, though for what reason she could not imagine. She couldn't tell what he was thinking, let alone why. His long sallow face with small eyes and thin nose was sour and secretive. Mrs Lipton wasn't much better, even though she did look more cheerful. She was always untidy – and none too clean, considering she had to handle the milk and cream and butter.

Upjohn remounted and rode out of the farmyard. She wasn't going to bother with the two farmhands. She didn't really consider them as part of the estate. 'Phew!' she said, thankful to escape from the whiffs of stables, cowstalls, pigsties and henhouses. She wouldn't like to have married a farmer!

She took a turning just beyond the farm and went down a narrow mud track leading to the little cottage where Jordan lived in the woods. Goodness knows how old he was, but he'd been no chicken when Upjohn first came and he was head keeper of the woods and the grouse moors beyond. She rarely set eyes on him now without remembering him as she had so often seen him in the past, walking in at the back door out of the chilly deep blue evening, limp birds dangling from his bloodied fingers, their beautiful brown and bronze feathers gleaming in the light which streamed through the scullery door.

Upjohn knocked at the cottage door and heard the old man's slippered feet whisper with surprising agility across the floor; then he stood in the doorway, peering a little to see who had called.

'Good morning, Mr Jordan.' A smile broke out across his face. 'I've come to see whether you'd like to give something towards a wreath for the Colonel?'

'Aye! That I will!' He went back into the living room to feel in a brown earthenware teapot on the mantelpiece for his money, and Upjohn, stepping inside the room and looking round, thought how very clean it was, seeing that the old man had lived alone for twelve years.

He held his hand out towards her. 'I wish it could be more,' he said. 'But me pension don't go far!'

All the same, his two half-crowns pressed solid into the palm of her hand felt a great deal more than the ten-shilling note Mr Lipton had held out to her at his fingertips.

'If you want to see the wreath,' she said, 'it'll be on his coffin in the library. Mr Harry asked me to pass the word round that everyone is welcome this afternoon at three o'clock.'

'I shall be there.' Jordan nodded his head several times, then closed the door gently as Upjohn moved away towards her bicycle.

As she rode back to the house she said to herself: there's a good old man. Simple, kind, clean-living. She'd never once heard him grumble or say a bad word. She wished there were more like him. That Lipton! Sour-faced old . . . Now Brown had an occasional grumble (about his lumbago and there not being enough help in the garden and all the hard work he had to do), but he was all right.

This was hard work if you liked. Pedalling up this road. Even after all these years she couldn't get used to the hilliness of Derbyshire; she came from the Cheshire plain herself.

Phew! She coasted along to the garage after a last turn of the pedals, which had seemed to grow steadily stiffer all the way up the drive.

She dismounted and propped herself up with her bicycle to get her breath.

The Rolls was standing in the garage. Streams of water had been drenched over it and were still running and spreading over the concrete floor. She could hear Matthews hissing between his teeth as he rubbed the car down with a wash-leather.

He appeared from behind it, still hissing and rubbing, glanced with bare concentration at her, and returned immediately to his task, working methodically and without haste along the sleek sides of the car until he came to the tip of the bonnet. He gave one final circular rub, then stood back and smiled with satisfaction at the gleaming black body.

'There, my beauty!'

Just as if it were a horse! How distressed he'd been, Upjohn remembered, when the carriage had been exchanged for a car. 'Give up my horses? Never!' he had declared. Yet here he was, as proud of his cars as he had ever been of his horses.

He came towards her, screwing the wash-leather between his hands, his short neat body rocking briefly, quickly, from side to side with the peculiarity of his walk.

He greeted her in his usual timid way. He seldom looked her straight in the face. After all these years! A married man he was, at that – although a widower now.

In response to her request he fumbled in his pocket and brought out a crumpled ten-shilling note, which he pushed

into her hand, snatching his own hand away quickly as though he had done something shameful.

'The coffin will be in the library if you want to come this afternoon – at three o'clock,' she told him, and to spur him to confidence she added: 'All the others are coming.'

'All right.'

He retreated into the back of the garage and all she could see of him then was the whiteness of his shirt moving about in the darkness.

She mounted her bicycle again to ride the short distance past the place where the chapel had been (pity they didn't clear away those old stones now) to the bicycle shed by the back door. She was thankful she had no further to ride. She got no younger, and that bike was stiff to pedal. All the same, she wasn't going to change it for one of these new-fangled things where you had to sit bent half-double over the handlebars – so undignified, cocked up like that at the back.

She went into the pantry and started to count the money.

Two pounds, eleven shillings. And she herself would make it up to three pounds. They should get a lovely wreath for that.

IV

At eleven o'clock sharp (Mr Harry didn't like to be kept wait-ing), the money carefully stowed away in her best black handbag, Upjohn stood at the pantry window watching for Mr Harry's car to come round to the front.

There he was! The car, pale grey and spotless, its chrome shining in the sun, glided slowly round the corner from the garage and pulled up smoothly by the front door.

Upjohn went out of the side door and across the courtyard.

How kind of Mr Harry to lean over from the driving seat and open the car door for her!

She climbed into the back seat and settled the handbag firmly across her knees.

'Successful?'

'Yes, Sir. Three pounds.'

'Well done!'

What flowers should she choose? The Colonel liked a bit of colour. But not gaudy. Nothing gaudy. That would not be suitable.

'You've told everyone they can come in this afternoon if they wish?'

'Yes, Sir.'

'Well done.'

He looked at the clock on the dashboard. His hand began to beat an impatient tattoo on the steering wheel. He gave a faint sigh. Then another, less faint. The minutes ticked past. At five past eleven he clicked his tongue with exasperation. Five minutes late already! Why *couldn't* people be punctual? Surely that wasn't too much to ask?

Upjohn was already beginning to watch the door uneasily, because impatience was bubbling up and up and might soon boil over, when to her relief Mr and Mrs Jack appeared.

'I'm sorry I'm late!' cried Laurine.

Jack leaned forward to open the back door of the car and

at the same time Harry stretched back from his seat, but before either of them could reach it Laurine had seized the handle of the front door, pulled it open and jumped into the seat beside Harry. She slammed the door after her.

Harry winced. 'These doors don't need to be slammed,' he reminded her.

'Oh, I'm sorry! I always forget. Silly me. But you see, sometimes if you don't slam doors they don't shut properly and then you might fall out. I very nearly did once, and my friend only grabbed me just in time. By my skirt.' She giggled and looked at Harry.

Harry merely repeated: 'These doors shut perfectly if they're shut gently. This happens to be a quality car.'

'Yes, of course. I'll try to remember, really I will.' She looked round to smile at Jack, installed in the back beside Upjohn.

They drove off.

'Why don't you have a radio in the car?' Laurine asked Harry.

'A wireless? Good heavens, no! That's one thing I most certainly should never have in my car. How can I concentrate on driving and listen to the wireless at the same time?'

'Oh, I should love listening to a radio in a car. Especially on a long drive, if I was all alone. And you don't need to concentrate if you're not going awfully fast, do you?'

'I never go awfully fast. And I always concentrate.'

Jack leaned over from the back to tell a story about going fast.

'Do you remember when the Old Boy – Father,' he amended hastily because of Upjohn, 'and that old brigadier friend of his were going to a show where my pictures were being exhibited, and I was driving them because Matthews had 'flu. I overheard the two old gentlemen in the back . . .'

'. . . telling each other that they couldn't understand the modern craze for speed and . . .' interjected Harry.

'. . . Father said he thought a steady thirty was quite fast enough, such as they were doing at that moment.' Jack took over the telling of his own story quite firmly because, even if Harry had heard it before, there was no reason why he should treat it as though it were his. 'And at that moment, had they but known it, they were doing sixty!'

Laurine burst out laughing. Upjohn smiled and looked out of the window. Jack sank back in his seat, chuckling at himself.

A car ahead slowed down with no warning, and Harry had to brake suddenly.

'Damned fool! Woman driver, I bet!' He changed gear and swerved past.

Laurine twisted round to look through the back window.

'No,' she said. 'It was a man!'

Harry made no comment.

'You're not going to park the car in the car park, are you?' asked Jack when they reached the shops.

'Of course! I think it's ridiculous to leave a car in the middle of the town where it may cause an obstruction. If you do, it's entirely your own fault if someone bumps into you. I don't want my car scratched and knocked about, thank you!'

'It always seems so silly to me to go and pay a couple of bob for the car park when you can park free in the main street.

Besides, it's such a hell of a way to walk. The florist's shop is right up the other end of the town.'

'Well, you've got a pair of legs!'

'Yes, you've got a pair of legs!' Laurine chipped in, laughing.

They got out of the car, which Harry had parked in the almost empty car park.

'You see – hardly anyone else trails down here to park their cars,' Jack said.

'I really don't care *what* other people do!' One after another Harry opened the three doors of the car, putting up the handles then shutting the doors firmly but gently so that the locks clicked. Then he closed the fourth door and locked it. He tried all the doors to make sure they were correctly locked, put the key in his pocket and set off towards the gateway marked EXIT. A brown canvas shopping bag was looped over his arm.

Jack glanced uneasily at the bag. 'What's that for?' he asked, pointing to it.

'I've got one or two things to do,' said Harry. He didn't enlarge upon them. He saw no reason why he should.

Only one bag, thank God – sometimes Harry brought two – but Jack knew that even one bag might mean an hour or more while Harry poked about the ironmonger's for tools and gadgets; the electrical shop for bits of wireless sets, plugs, adaptors, God-knew-what; the wool shop for crochet cotton; the bookshop; the library . . .

'I'm just going to slip across the road,' said Laurine, catching sight of the array of bottles and jars in the window of the hairdresser's opposite. She was getting low in her stock of cosmetics. If she had a look in that window it would remind her of what she needed, and perhaps on the way back she could get Jack to have a look too. 'I'll catch you up,' she said, and hurried across the street.

'I just have to go in here to collect a pair of shoes for Mrs Winthorpe,' said Upjohn, turning into the shoe shop. Harry nodded, and he and Jack continued on up the street alone.

'It's good of the old girl to go round like that collecting for a wreath,' said Jack. 'We'll have to thank them all. I think it would be a good idea if I went round personally. I think they appreciate that sort of thing.'

'Oh, I daresay they'd *appreciate* it. . . .'

'Do you think I might borrow your car? It takes such a hell of a time going down to the farm and up to the gardens on foot.'

Borrow the Bentley? The very idea! 'I never lend my car to anyone,' said Harry firmly.

'But I'd only be using it where there was no traffic. However, if you would rather I didn't, perhaps you wouldn't mind driving me round? It wouldn't take long.'

The dust on the farm road would get all over the car. The ruts would be bad for tyres and springs.

'I really do think it's unnecessary to go round in person,' Harry said. 'I can write a note for circulation. Or you can,' he conceded. 'If you'd rather.'

'I think I should. I'm the eldest, after all, and they'd expect it.'

'I really don't think they'd expect anything. And anyway, I have lived here all my life, as you know. Still, if you want to do

it, do it. Only in my opinion it's not neccessary for anyone to go round in person. Why not thank them this afternoon when they come to the private view?'

'Well . . . yes . . . possibly . . .' What an extraordinary expression to use! Jack thought. Almost as if Father were at the Royal Academy. When's varnishing day?

Laurine crossed back from her window-gazing with a well-filled list in her mind, and started to follow Jack and Harry. She could see them further up the street, going quite slowly, Jack's hat bobbing along over the heads of the people and the rest of them now appearing, now disappearing, as the stream of passers-by thinned and thickened: Jack tall and rather smart, Harry not quite so tall and not quite so smart, with the old brown canvas bag dangling from his fingers almost to the ground.

The florist's was just ahead now, just beyond the traffic lights. Jack and Harry were turning in at the door.

There might be orchids in the shop, thought Laurine. And sprays of gardenias, bunches of violets, single crimson or pink or yellow roses pinned perhaps round a mirror on an oval velvet blackboard.

She quickened her steps.

V

As they left the dining room after lunch Mrs Winthorpe suddenly paused, right in the doorway. Laurine, following close behind, had to pull up sharply to avoid bumping into her.

'Did you all get nice wreaths?' Mrs Winthorpe said to Harry, who was holding the door open for her.

'Adequate.'

'Oh? You mean they didn't have anything very nice?'

'I don't mean anything of the sort. They had a very adequate selection.' He rattled the door handle.

'I was afraid that perhaps at such short notice . . . although Joanna and I . . . Still, you're really satisfied with what you got?'

'Yes, yes,' Jack broke in. Good Lord, why on earth couldn't she get a move on! Standing in the doorway like that holding up the traffic (and he was at the end of the queue). One felt such a fool, with Upjohn hovering about in the background like a black crow.

'We got some beautiful flowers!' Laurine said brightly. 'Harry chose irises, and Jack and I . . .'

Jack nudged her. He frowned at her enquiring glance and shook his head to stop her carrying on about the flowers. They'd be here all day else. Why *must* Mother make a habit of these stops for conversation by the wayside?

'Oh, well, I'm glad you're satisfied,' said Mrs Winthorpe, thinking vaguely that Laurine's voice had ceased rather abruptly, but without trying to guess the reason. She hadn't really been listening anyway. One didn't really listen to Laurine. . . .

Harry rattled the handle again, shook the door a little so as to dislodge and pass her through the doorway.

She moved on.

Thankfully they followed her.

She suddenly stopped again in the middle of the passage to the drawing room. 'I hope the flowers will be here before – before *he* is!'

'They said they'd send them up directly after lunch, with the ones you and Joanna chose yesterday.' Harry sidestepped her neatly so as to turn off up the stairs and retire to his room for his afternoon nap.

'For God's sake be down before he *does* come back!' Jack called after him.

'I shall be down in half an hour,' said Harry firmly. No later; but not a minute sooner.

'Well, I only hope that *will* be before he comes.'

Harry went on upstairs in silence and Jack glowered at the broad, grey, gradually-disappearing behind. Going off for a nap like that and leaving them to cope with the flowers! And to get Mother moving into the drawing room; perhaps even to cope with the coffin . . .

'Oh, Good God!' he exclaimed. 'Harry!'

The feet paused, on the third flight.

'What is it now?'

Jack ran upstairs two steps at a time; behind him, Mrs Winthorpe's fading voice serenely continued speaking her original thought: 'If they're here first, we can put the lilies about the room while we're still – while the library is still – empty. . . .'

'Harry!' Jack struggled to get breath, heartbeats loud in his eardrums. While getting back his breath, he took time off from the thought which had precipitated him upstairs to assure himself that he was still pretty fit on the whole. After all, it was three flights, and he'd taken them at the gallop.

When his breathing had slowed down, he said: 'They won't leave the lid off, will they?'

'Lid? What lid?'

'Lid of the coffin – so people could come and take a look – if they wanted to?' He was very anxious.

'No, of course not! Naturally not. I told them to screw it down.' Harry drew his lips together and frowned severely at Jack. What on earth did Jack think he was.

'Oh, that's all right! I only wanted to make sure.'

Harry continued on his way. He supposed that eventually he would be allowed to reach his room.

Jack walked downstairs again, slowly, relaxed with relief. His legs descended loosely from step to step. It would have been ghastly not to have had the lid screwed down. But one never knew. It was better to make sure.

Laurine and Mrs Winthorpe were still standing at the foot of the stairs. Mrs Winthorpe was picking her thumb.

'What is it?' she asked as Jack joined them.

'Nothing, nothing,' he replied and got behind her. Perhaps he could somehow tip her gently towards the drawing room where at least they would be able to sit down. His knees felt quite weak.

'I was just saying to Laurine that we must get the vases out ready for the lilies. Joanna *would* make me get Madonna lilies to put in the library. I hope they're suitable. All white seemed somehow . . . however, they do smell delicious. . . .'

'Divine!' agreed Laurine, and catching Jack's eye she edged slightly in the direction of the drawing room.

'Besides . . .' said Mrs Winthorpe.

Oh, God! How much longer? thought Jack. This slowness of getting from pillar to post was driving him crazy. It seemed to hinder the process, hold things up – so that they would never get to the funeral and never, never get to the reading of the will.

'. . . the library is so dark, the lilies will light it up. And, of course, there are the yellow roses with them, I'd forgotten those. Personally, I've always thought it a very gloomy room. But *he* liked it, so I suppose . . .'

Jack wanted to wave his arms at her and make shushing noises as one did at geese. . . . But one could not possibly drive Mother as one might drive geese. One must just encourage. . . .

He shuffled his feet backwards and forwards on the carpet.

'Shall Jack and I go and get the vases now?' Laurine suggested.

Jack grabbed Laurine's hand and made off with her towards the china cupboard. Mrs Winthorpe's voice followed them: 'Yes. Yes, do. You know where they are. . . .'

Mrs Winthorpe moved on towards the drawing room, alone. Just outside the drawing room door she stopped again. Was that a motor coming up the drive? Her heart began to pound and she half started to hurry back towards the china cupboard, making the excuse that perhaps Jack and Laurine would not be able to find the right vases. Then she stopped herself and went resolutely to the window which overlooked the drive.

Oh, thank goodness! It was a bright green van. That couldn't possibly be him! That would be the flowers. She quite

loved it, the cheerful little green van, rattling up to the back door to unload its armfuls of scent and colour.

She walked back towards the china cupboard, quite slowly this time, calling out gaily: 'The flowers have come!'

Jack emerged with a vase in each hand.

'Look, Mother,' he said. 'These are the only two glass ones that Laurine thinks would be large enough, and there are two white pottery ones. There are also one or two large pink pottery ones. Would they do?'

'Oh, I should . . . I don't know. . . .' She peered into the cupboard at them a little doubtfully. Where on earth had all her vases got to? They were awfully short of vases suddenly.

She made up her mind. 'Yes, I think they'll do. After all, they're only a very *pale* pink. Bring them along to the flower room, will you?'

They watched her set off along the passage again, and this time she went without a halt, sailing straight for the flower room.

VI

In silence they gathered in the library and looked around with satisfaction.

The white lilies, arranged in vases (none of which looked too pink), shone against the sombre leather-bound books which lined the walls of the entire room. Father's great leather-topped desk and leather chair had been pushed from their customary place in the centre of the room into a corner.

Behind them, the bronze bust of Grandfather surveyed them from its pedestal like a benign Moses.

Wrightson's had been (but not until Harry had come down from his nap, mercifully), and the light-coloured oak coffin, screwed down securely, rested in place on the trestles in the centre of the room. A wreath of red roses lay upon it. The rest of the flowers were grouped on a dustsheet spread on the floor beneath it.

'I'm glad I had those red roses!' whispered Mrs Winthorpe. 'They aren't too bright, but they do lend colour. We must keep them away from Joanna's bronze irises. They'll kill each other.'

'Yes,' Jack replied in a whisper. He wondered if he could paint a picture of this. He wasn't very good at interiors. Still, he'd have a shot.

'I hope they won't fade before tomorrow. We must sprinkle them with water, keep them moist.'

Jack narrowed his eyes, composing the blocks of colour into a satisfactory form – yes – an impressionistic picture, he thought, nothing too defined: the white flowers, the dark greens and browns and rusts of the books, the smooth coffin like a big violin, the bronze bust of Grandfather overlooking all. He ought to have that bust now, he thought. He was the eldest son.

'Nothing looks worse than droopy flowers!' Mrs Winthorpe hissed.

'Why do we all keep whispering?' asked Jack. He spoke a little more loudly.

'I don't know,' Mrs Winthorpe replied, speaking a little

louder herself. 'I suppose one just does it naturally. . . .' She glanced at the coffin.

'We'd better shift that cabinet away from the window.' Harry spoke in his normal voice and Mrs Winthorpe and Jack looked at him admiringly. 'It blocks the light where it is.'

'Yes,' said Mrs Winthorpe, 'it does. And this is such a gloomy room anyway.' Her voice gained in strength as she spoke.

Harry and Jack took hold of the walnut cabinet, one at each end, lifting it very carefully, but in spite of their care shaking it slightly, so that the glass shelves and the things upon them rattled as they carried it away from the window.

'Aren't they lovely, those things?' said Laurine, peering through the glass doors at the objects inside.

Sometimes, secretly, when Father had been out of the way, she had slipped in to gaze at them and think which ones she would have chosen if by any miracle he had said to her: 'You may take whichever you want.'

There was the darling little enamel watch, blue and gold, to hang on one's lapel; a necklace of coral which would look wonderful on a black dress; another necklace of carved ivory and yet another of gold coins; a bronze butterfly head ornament; a yellow wooden paper knife on which two painted swallows flew towards each other above the word 'Biarritz'; a bright orange leather belt with a huge buckle – it would just go round her waist (her waist was slim, thank goodness, although the rest of her was, as Jack said, 'Just plump enough!' which was exactly as it should be).

Mrs Winthorpe came up beside her.

'Oh, such a lot of junk!' she said. 'What are we going to do with all that junk? He collected such queer things when he was serving abroad . . . I never could understand . . . those ivory figures and shells and native ornaments and weapons and things.'

Laurine saw Father walking abroad, barefoot along a beach, with trousers rolled up from blue waves rippling white ribbons along a stretch of sand, stooping to gather those shells: the big shallow curved one with the inside shimmering like a rainbow; the pale pink one with deeper pink inside and funny spikes sticking out all over it like long warts; the shiny silvery-white one like a great snail. And brown natives, naked but for beads (would he have been shocked?) brought him gifts of the knives and the necklaces; laughing girls with bare breasts hung festoons of brilliant flowers round his neck, over his khaki shirt.

'I never could see the point of those necklaces. They're so gaudy. Nobody could possibly wear them. And that butterfly! He made it for me himself when we were engaged. To wear in my hair. As if I *could* have! Imagine!'

She stopped talking suddenly and glanced uneasily at the coffin, only a few feet away.

Laurine looked at her, trying to imagine her loved by Father, trying to see Father's devotion pouring over her like rich cream before it turned sour – when he still wanted to bring gifts to please her, to make things for her. Father abroad was easy to see: he was a stranger then, in a foreign country, and one could imagine him as one wished. But at home . . . she tried in vain to see him young and handsome, on one knee offering gifts, saying 'Will you?' The cross old man kept rising up before her and ruining the chances of the nice young man.

'The wreath from the servants is rather good, isn't it?' said Jack, turning his back on the cabinet. He knew Laurine coveted those things, and it didn't seem quite right somehow . . . with the Old Boy in the room. . . .

'Lovely,' agreed Mrs Winthorpe, joining him beside the coffin. She dropped her voice to a whisper again. 'And so are yours and Laurine's and Harry's. I expect Brian and Elizabeth will bring theirs with them when they come this evening. . . .'

She walked round to have one more look at all the flowers, sighed, and said forlornly: 'What shall we do now? Shall we go and sit in the drawing room?'

'Well, *I* certainly haven't got time to sit in the drawing room,' said Harry. 'I've got things to see to.'

'The people on the place will be coming in soon, won't they?' said Mrs Winthorpe. 'We don't want to embarrass them by all being here.'

'No,' said Jack. 'Not all of us. But I think *I* ought to be here. They'll expect it. They'll probably all come in a bunch, weeping and wailing and gnashing their teeth,' he added.

'Nonsense!' said Harry, so loudly that Mrs Winthorpe glanced at him uneasily. Alfred?

'Oh, no! Surely not?' she said.

'Well, that class, you know . . .' Jack persisted.

'But still . . .' said Mrs Winthorpe.

'Anyway, *I'm* going now.' Harry turned away.

As they walked past the front door they saw the little group of servants in the courtyard.

'Foregathering!' Harry remarked.

'What did I tell you?' said Jack.

'They won't want to see *me*, will they?' Mrs Winthorpe enquired anxiously.

'I can't think of any reason why they should,' said Harry.

'I had a very nice note from Mrs Lipton this morning. Although I don't care for her at all . . . she never looks clean and I hate to think of her making my butter. I always try *not* to think of it! And Lipton always looks so disagreeable. He's so very . . .' She looked for the word, found it, and produced it triumphantly: 'Taciturn! I never could see why Father insisted on keeping him all this time. . . .'

'Because he's a good bailiff, that's why.' Surely that was obvious, thought Harry.

'But so disagreeable.'

'Well, that's not really the point.'

'I suppose . . . after all, as you say, he *is* a good . . . and these days, I suppose . . .'

Laurine watched her irresolute, wavering, like the flame of a candle in a strong draught.

'. . . and Mrs Lipton did write a very nice note. I had one from Brown, too,' Mrs Winthorpe continued. 'All the Heads ought to write, of course.' She was burning steadily again now. 'But I don't suppose Matthews will. He's so shy. It's very foolish of him to be so shy. And he's not a good driver. Too nervous. Although he was wonderful with the horses in the old days.'

'Well, you could do a lot worse than Lipton *or* Matthews.' Harry frowned. 'You must realise that.'

'Oh, I do! I do!' Mrs Winthorpe protested quickly. Harry must not get the impression that she was complaining. She was not complaining. Not. She was just saying what she thought. And everyone was entitled to do that . . . weren't they?

The little group in the courtyard broke up for a moment, drew together again, elongated and started to file towards the house, headed by Upjohn.

'My God, I'd better get back to the library!' said Jack. 'She's taking them in by the French window to avoid bringing them through the house. I must be there when they come in. They'll expect it.'

He started off at a brisk trot.

I'm sure they won't, Harry told himself.

Jack turned back. He had suddenly remembered Laurine.

'You'll stay with Mother, won't you, darling?' He gave her a quick squeeze, said: 'See you later' and skipped off to the library to take up his position by the coffin just as Upjohn came in through the window.

He wondered what they were thinking about as they filed in after Upjohn: Mrs Brown, Mrs Lipton, Mrs Burton, Mrs Bannister, stepping carefully over the shallow ledge which separated the rough grey flagstones of the terrace from the smooth honeyed surface of the oak floor.

They trod slowly, carefully, on tiptoes, as they crossed the floorboards. When they reached the carpet their heels sank with relief into silence.

Mrs Brown looked more wizened and grey than ever. Her little wrinkled face peered out from beneath the straw of her hat like that of a sad, brown-eyed monkey. That idiot son must

cause her a lot of worry! It was clever how they always seemed to manage to keep him under control.

Mrs Lipton was enormous beside Mrs Brown, and as untidy as ever. Her face was red and shining, wisps of tow-coloured hair escaped from beneath the tattered and faded blue felt hat over her lined forehead. One wisp, an especially long one, straggled down her right cheek and every now and then she raised a hand to brush it away. Upjohn glanced at Mrs Lipton and Jack read her thought: 'Is that woman wiping her eyes? Is she going to give way?'

He was sure that Upjohn, having organised things so far, was taking upon herself the responsibility of seeing that everyone behaved as they should. Old dragon!

He noticed that all the women, with the exception of Mrs Bannister, had come with their heads covered. Even Mrs Burton had perched a dark purple straw hat on top of her white hair; it looked queer, because she still had on her apron which from time to time she picked up and, in spite of Upjohn's warning glances, dabbed gently over her eyes.

God knew why. She had only been with the family eighteen months. Probably thought it the thing to do.

How Mother would disapprove of Mrs Bannister coming hatless. 'Fancy coming without a hat' she would say in a whisper (which she really believed to be inaudible), quite forgetting that both she and Laurine were hatless. Dear old lady, she was so inconsistent! Bless her!

The men, keeping their distance, came in a little way behind the women. The continuous tread of their feet across the oak boards was almost startling in the silence.

Lipton, ignoring Jack completely, looked straight ahead of him at the coffin, glumly. Yes, he certainly was *not* a pleasant man – even if he was a good bailiff.

Matthews came in, a few yards behind Lipton and Brown, rocking over the boards with that priceless walk of his, his feet tapping so briskly that Upjohn leaned from behind the stoutness of Mrs Burton to give him one of her looks. But Matthews missed it because he was, as usual, avoiding everybody's eyes by keeping his own eyes on the cap which he was twirling round and round in his hands. How like a tortoise he was! That queer, mild, blunt little face stretched slightly forwards on its skinny neck was always ready to draw back into its shell at the slightest hint of a snub.

Mother was right about Matthews, too, Matthews was murder as a driver. Jamming on the brakes if he saw a chicken crossing the road half a mile off; blowing the horn at every corner; slowing down to fifteen through the thirties; waiting for every other car on the road when it was his right-of-way. And worse still, if one was driving with him beside one – on the rare occasions one *was* able to drive the Rolls (though come to think of it, old Harry seemed to get away with it quite a bit), 'Steady, Sir!' Steady, Sir!' Steady, now!'

He lost his shyness then, became busy and bossy, just as he had when he was a young groom teaching Harry to ride. How he used to rant at poor old Harry, who always hated horses. 'Grip with your knees, now, Master 'arry! *Grip!* Let the reins go slack! Don't pull on 'is 'ead like that! Lord, you'll ruin 'is mouth!' And finally, in utter disappointment and disgust: 'You'll never 'ave a seat, Master 'arry, and that's a fact!'

Last in the procession came old Jordan. He stopped outside the window and took his pipe out of his mouth, knocked
it against the wall and put it in his pocket. Then he removed
his hat and stepped inside. As he joined the others he touched
his forehead to Jack. Next to him, Jim Bobbett, who had
omitted to do so before, hastily followed his example.

Jack felt a warm glow spread through him.

The women moved nearer to the coffin. They fanned out
a little and started to flow round it. The men followed the
women. There was silence except for an occasional whisper
from one of the women, hushed, or a deep murmur from a
man. . . .

A sudden shadow fell on the room. Everyone looked
towards the open window.

Tommy Brown stood outside, dumbly, his hands twisting
together.

'I'm sorry, Sir,' Brown whispered to Jack. 'I'd no idea he
could get here. We left him indoors.'

'It's all right. Let him come in if he wants to.'

Brown went quickly to Tommy, took the cap off his head
and gave it to him to hold, then led him gently to his mother's
side.

'Naughty boy, Tommy!' she whispered lovingly.

Jack felt a wave of pity and horror surge over him at the
sight of this middle-aged man, only six years younger than
himself, being treated like a child, who even had the face of a
child: no wrinkles marking the dull, greyish-white skin; only
the faintest down darkening the skin above the thick upper
lip and growing rather more abundantly over the round skull:

the eyes quite innocent, uncomprehending and uncomplaining. Mucus gleaming from nostril to upper lip, like the track of a snail.

Docilely, Tommy let himself be led by his mother while the pretty flowers were pointed out to him. An occasional grunt, a blundering incoherent attempt at speech (who is in that box, perhaps?) burst from him into the quiet whispers and murmurs and muffled footsteps shuffling round the room.

As Jordan drew abreast, Jack leaned forward to greet him. From the old man's calm blue eyes shone the acknowledgement, the respect, which Jack was sure Jordan had always felt towards him, towards the family. Here, at least, was one who acknowledged the superiority of master over servant, whose respect had not passed with the passing of the good old days.

Upjohn, standing near the window, rounded up every member of her flock as they completed the tour round the coffin. She formed them into a small herd, and ushered them, one by one, out through the window. Each of the men turned to salute Jack. Last of all went Upjohn, closing the window carefully after her.

As Jack watched them disappear, sudden deep grief seized him. This was the end. The past lay dead, sealed in that wooden box. These people, these men and women who for so many years had been a part of this estate, had said their last farewell not only to their master but to their familiar life. Soon that, too, would be scattered into new places and new days – the old days were gone for ever.

If the old custom had been followed, if times had not changed, all these people would now be in *his* service, Jack

thought. They would have belonged to him, as the house should have belonged to him. The king is dead: long live the king! *He was the eldest son.*

VII

How nice to have the whole family together again, said Mrs Winthorpe to herself as she preceded them into the dining room for dinner.

She sailed to her place at the foot of the table, and watched all the members of the family – except, of course, Alfred! – follow one another into the room and fan out to surround the table.

Jack, the eldest son, sat opposite her now, in Alfred's place at the head of the table, Laurine on his right; dear Elizabeth on his left. . . .

'We can't separate all the husbands and wives,' Mrs Winthorpe said, as she sat down. 'It comes all wrong. . . .'

. . . Joanna next to Elizabeth (two women together, that wasn't right either), then Harry on her own right hand and Tony on her left (that was nice because he always talked to her and Harry was rather silent); and next to Tony was Brian and then Laurine . . . but she needn't go round the table again!

Upjohn finished handing the plates of soup.

It was iced tomato soup with whipped cream, and Mrs Winthorpe thought it looked quite hideous against the mauve flowers in the centre of the table (if there were such things as black flowers, she really did believe Upjohn would have put them there!); she hoped it would all be eaten up quickly and

cleared away. Personally, she didn't care much for soup, especially thick soup, especially *cold*. It seemed to fill one up so, but Brian liked it. . . .

'What delicious soup, Grandmama,' said Tony, setting out to make conversation. He thought it damned rude of Harry just to sit in silence. All the same, his own mind was not on the soup at all. It was on Joanna. What the hell was the matter with her now? She seemed more on edge than ever – and it'd hardly be because the old man had kicked the bucket. Or would it? What must his next move be?

'Yes, yes, it is delicious soup. It's tomato!' she explained unnecessarily.

Joanna glanced at her grandmother, wondering how she felt at no longer seeing, after all these years (more than fifty of them, day in, day out), the same face opposite. What a terrible thing it was when love turned to indifference – or worse. Nothing shared, no companionship, no laughter, no loving-kindness. She looked at Tony's thin lips under the well-groomed moustache. Loving-kindness! Her heart ached and she remembered Andrew's hands . . . his mouth . . . that day on the river, the last day she had spent with him . . . a day of hot sun and cool water and love on hidden islands.

And at the day's end, when the sun was already starting to go down, they had eaten bread and cheese outside a little riverside inn. Boats passed up and down the river before them: small boats with couples nestling in them; cabin cruisers with families aboard preparing for the oncoming night; swift launches; the river steamer filled with happy people singing in the gathering dusk.

Behind the bench where they sat to watch the boats a blue-flowered plant curved up the white wall of the inn. The door of the bar-parlour stood open and through the thin veil of smoke glowed an orange light peopled with dark living silhouettes. Muffled voices drifted out on the warmth from the open door; clear voices drifted up on the evening coolness from the river. A small black cat came on knowing, silent paws, and leapt lightly onto Joanna's knee. Curling itself round and round with delicate grace, it nestled in her lap.

Andrew said: 'Perhaps it will bring us luck.' He touched it gently and his hand rested for a moment on the little cat asleep in her lap.

A distant accordion sounded softly across the water, the gay lilt saddened with a subtle melancholy barely perceptible. Someone started to sing.

And still, while the twilight deepened to dusk, and the dusk to night, the boats passed smoothly along the river, their little lights shining above and reflected in the water below, and the voices continued to weave their music through the air – warm voices, kindly voices, the voices of comrades . . . .

The voices grew louder, became actual, became the voices of the family seated round the dining table in the candlelight.

Mrs Winthorpe saw the wistfulness softening Joanna's face. What a good thing. Joanna's face had seemed so hard sometimes lately, almost bitter.

Still keeping an ear open for Tony's conversation (she was listening) which had somehow passed from soup to zombies (however had they travelled all the way to South Africa?), Mrs

Winthorpe smiled at Joanna, and the fleeting tenderness was arrested and developed into an answering smile.

Tony saw the secret smile and said to Mrs Winthorpe: 'You have a very beautiful granddaughter.' He wondered angrily to himself why the hell Joanna was looking so happy just then.

'What?' said Mrs Winthorpe.

He would go and say something sweet and blue-eyed like that in public, thought Joanna angrily, the smile dying quickly from her face. They ought to see him sometimes in private, sometimes when the mask had slipped. In the back of her mind fluttered the thought that she ought to unmask him in public, she ought to have the strength. What would they say? She imagined one by one their shocked faces. And Andrew? What would they say about Andrew?

'You have a very beautiful granddaughter,' Tony repeated, more slowly, carefully placing the accent on the 'very'.

'Oh, yes! Yes!' Mrs Winthorpe laughed and flushed. A compliment to one of her family was a compliment to herself (she had produced them, hadn't she?) – except when that common little man at Torquay, what was his name now? Whoopee George, she thought they called him, of all ridiculous things, had asked her how she managed to produce such a gorgeous creature as Joanna. Such cheek! She had been very cool to him after that. Such cheek!

'Very beautiful,' Tony said for the third time.

There! thought Harry. It was quite obvious the chap cared for her, whatever Brian might say.

Upjohn came in bearing a silver platter on which lay a neat leg of mutton.

Mrs Winthorpe stretched her neck to scrutinise it as it passed her on its way to the sideboard. Was it done enough?

Harry rose. Jack rose. They looked at each other.

Jack said graciously: 'You go ahead and carve, Harry, old man, if you'd like to. You're a good deal more expert at it than I am. We seldom run to a joint in our household.' He sat down again. 'Do we, darling?' He held out his hand for Laurine's.

'Is it pink?' said Mrs Winthorpe anxiously, as Harry started to carve. Oh, dear! He had got his table napkin tucked into his waistcoat – just like Alfred!

'No. Why should it be?'

'Well, sometimes she doesn't do things quite enough . . . I can't bear underdone mutton. I don't call Mrs Burton a very good cook really,' she added, as Upjohn went out of the room to fetch the vegetables. 'Do you?' she appealed to Brian.

But it was Harry who answered her: 'Nonsense! She's a good plain cook!'

'You're always grumbling!' Mrs Winthorpe jumped. Had *Harry* actually said that? No, no! Harry hadn't said it at all. It was Alfred's voice. And, of course, it was only in her imagination.

'A very small piece for me, please,' she said, adding meekly: 'when it's my turn.'

Brian watched Harry carve. *He* didn't want only a very small piece. He was hungry.

Mrs Winthorpe muttered in an undertone not for Harry's ears: 'These plates are cold again.' Her fingers danced a melancholy jig on the plate in front of her.

Jack started to mould his bread meticulously into pellets and place them one after another in a row in front of him while he waited for his mutton.

Tony saw them and felt suddenly unbearably irritated, and even more irritated that he was unable to discover the exact cause of his irritation. Bread balls. Bread balls? What was wrong with bread balls?

He turned to Brian, having decided that it was now time to talk to him.

'Well, how's business these days, Brian?' he said, adopting the usual genial, man-to-man attitude he put on for Brian. He was as good as Brian any day (better, in fact). 'Working your usual wonders?'

Brian shovelled peas and potatoes onto his plate. There weren't a great many left, so he took the lot.

'I landed a contract for four hundred tractors from Brazil last month . . .' he began.

'Ah!' Tony interrupted. 'But will you be able to produce them?'

'Of course we shall!' said Brian, his voice rising in a melody of pained surprise. No, he was sure Tony was not all that Harry seemed to think he was.

So clever, thought Mrs Winthorpe. Somebody – was it Harry? – had once passed the remark that Brian had been very lucky to land that job. But Mrs Winthorpe knew it wasn't luck. It was brains. And, of course, hard work (the 7.55). Fancy selling four hundred tractors in one month! *She* couldn't do that. . . . It wasn't tough, was it, this mutton (lamb!)? She turned it over and over in her mouth, trying to make up her mind.

She couldn't imagine why Harry would insist that Mrs Burton was a good cook. She was not a good cook! Harry seemed to enjoy contradicting. She felt aggrieved.

'Do *you* think Mrs Burton is a good cook?' She sent a sudden appeal to Elizabeth.

'I don't – well, no – perhaps – I haven't really had an awful lot of her cooking,' Elizabeth glanced at Harry but he was not looking at her, so she felt encouraged enough to shake her head at Mrs Winthorpe, quite definitely.

'The other day she sent in a rice pudding that had about three grains of rice in it. The rest was milk,' Mrs Winthorpe went on, made bold by Harry's apparent oblivion. 'Ridiculous.'

'Fiendish,' Elizabeth agreed.

'You could do a great deal worse,' said Harry, as sharply as he could with a mouthful of mutton which he was not going to admit was tough.

He was very annoyed with them for deserving the reproach. He had far more important things to think about than how many grains of rice there were in a pudding. So had they, if only they realised it, he thought, glancing at Joanna. They were all on the brink of a family scandal!

The swing door from the pantry opened and the great Persian cat, Nebuchadnezzar, came in. He stalked along without a single glance to either side of him. When he reached the head of the table he paused and looked up. Jack held out his hand. Nebuchadnezzar stretched his neck slightly towards the hand, and his whiskers trembled a little as he sniffed the fingertips. Then he turned his back and walked away.

Mrs Winthorpe said: 'He always used to go straight to Father's chair and sit up for him to scratch the back of his head. He won't take any notice of anyone else.'

'The Old Boy used to love that cat,' said Brian.

'Yes. He always spoke kindly to Nebuchadnezzar!' said Mrs Winthorpe rather bitterly.

Harry glanced down to the end of the table – at Jack, sitting in Father's place. Strange to think how the Old Man's voice had droned on through the years and one actually noticed it more now that it was silenced – like a clock whose tick was so familiar that one only became aware of it after it had stopped. He sighed and laid his knife and fork tidily together on his plate. Although the clock had ceased to tick, things must go on as before . . . Father's wishes must be carried out. Father's will must be done. He was Father's right-hand man. Father depended on him. He looked at Joanna, thoughtfully, then across the table at Tony.

The remains of the leg of mutton were carried out by Upjohn. As a concession, for there were eight of them and Upjohn had her work cut out, Harry collected the used plates, vegetable dishes, gravy and sauceboats on a tray and carried them out to the pantry.

As he disappeared through the swing door Mrs Winthorpe leaned across to Tony and said in a defiant whisper: 'There wasn't enough mint in the sauce. It was nearly all vinegar.'

Tony turned from Brian and the tractors long enough to send a smiling glance to Mrs Winthorpe which put her perfectly in the right and utterly condemned Mrs Burton as a cook.

Mrs Winthorpe sighed with pleasure. It was nice to have a little support. And Harry was so. . . . Although, of course, cooks – good cooks – were hard to come by. Should she, or should she not, give Mrs Burton notice?

Harry came back and heavily sat himself in his chair again. He resumed his pondering.

Joanna continued to stare ahead of her in silence.

'You're very quiet, Miss,' said Mrs Winthorpe.

Joanna frowned. She was conscious of the sudden switch of attention to herself. They were all looking her way now, watching her. It was as if that battery of eyes was searching her, probing through her defences, lighting on Andrew within her.

Oh dear, thought Mrs Winthorpe. Couldn't one even make a joke? What was the matter with everyone?

How unhappy Joanna looked, thought Elizabeth. She couldn't bear to see anyone unhappy, when she herself was so happy. To fill the awkward silence she said: 'We ran into Myra Lorne at a party the other day, you remember her, don't you, Joanna?'

But it was Mrs Winthorpe who answered. 'Myra Lorne?' she said. 'Myra Lorne? Oh, yes, *that* little creature! Oh, I was so afraid in the old days that Brian was going to marry her!' She glanced at Brian, but he was fully occupied driving tractors round the world for Tony's benefit. 'She was after him, you know,' she went on. 'I wouldn't have cared for that at all! She was five foot nothing. Such an insignificant little . . .' She pulled herself up quickly and glanced at Laurine to see if she was listening. She was.

Brian, who had caught the last part of the conversation, covered up the *faux pas*. 'Good things are often done up in small parcels, you know, Mother.'

Tony forced a laugh.

'Wasn't Myra Lorne the one who went to Switzerland to have a baby before she was married?' asked Joanna.

'Oh!' said Mrs Winthorpe, shocked. 'Do you mean she had a – a blowfly?'

They looked at her in puzzled silence. Blowfly? *Blowfly?*

Then Harry exclaimed impatiently: 'By-blow! By-blow!' Really, Mother's unworldliness was beyond anything at times!

'Oh, yes,' said Mrs Winthorpe gratefully. 'I knew it began with a B!'

Laurine giggled and Elizabeth frowned at her, gently.

'What a long time Upjohn is,' Mrs Winthorpe grumbled. The conversation about Myra Lorne and her blowfly – by-blow – had flown out of her reach. Tony had turned back to Brian, and she was soon going to be bored.

'Well, Upjohn can't fly, you know,' Harry pointed out.

Laurine giggled again as she pictured Upjohn on the wing.

'No, I suppose not,' said Mrs Winthorpe. And it's cheese soufflé, and that always holds things up – oh, here she comes.'

Brian bent low over his plate to sniff the delicious cheesy smell. He began to eat. 'Wonderful, Mother,' he said.

'Is it light?'

'Light as a fart!'

'Brian!' Really, Brian came out with some awful things at times – and he'd been brought up so carefully. Tony pre-

tended not to have heard. Mrs Winthorpe looked round to see if anyone else had heard what she knew was only meant for her, just to shock her. At the table too! All the same, Mrs Burton's soufflé was as light as a . . . feather.

'Mrs Burton makes very good soufflés,' Mrs Winthorpe pronounced. 'It's about the only thing she does do really well.'

Harry opened his mouth to protest; then closed it again. It wasn't worthwhile.

Silence fell. The soufflé vanished, spoonful by spoonful.

'Doesn't it seem funny without Father?' Laurine's voice rang out high and clear.

They all looked at her, startled. What a thing for her to say, all of a sudden like that.

It brought Father right into their very midst. His voice sounded in every ear.

It seemed to Jack as though Father were sitting in the very chair he himself was occupying. Father's own chair: Father was sitting with him; under him; on him. . . . Almost he *was* Father; and yet he was horribly not.

Mrs Winthorpe had an urge not to stay in this room a moment longer. 'Shall we go?' She stood up.

'What about the port?' said Harry.

Brian looked up. Port? They hadn't had port for years. Father hadn't produced any since the war. Said he was too hard up.

Mrs Winthorpe sat down again in her chair with a sigh.

Harry went over to the sideboard, unlocked it and brought out a decanter. Brian and Jack eyed the deep-ruby liquid with approval.

'The Old Man had been hoarding this stuff for years,' said Harry complacently, as he held the decanter up to the light. 'It'll be useless if it isn't drunk soon.'

'Oh, it's the Old Man's, is it?' said Brian.

'Well, of course it's the Old Man's!' said Harry. Whoever else's would it be? Really, Brian was . . . 'At least,' he went on, 'it *was* the Old Man's. But he said he wished all the wine to be divided up equally among the three of us, so it's ours now.'

'He didn't tell *me* that,' said Brian.

'He didn't tell *me* he wanted to be cremated,' Harry retorted.

Brian was silent.

All the same, he wondered what Father was going to say to them guzzling his port while he was still . . . among them . . . not really as far away as the library . . . no, he was here, in this very room.

'Er – I don't know whether I . . .' he began.

'Laurine?' Harry poised the decanter over her glass.

'No! No, thank you!' She gave a little shriek and covered her glass with her fingers. 'Not port!' She looked up at Harry through her eyelashes and laughed. But he had already passed on.

'Jack?'

'Yes, please. Rather!'

'Elizabeth?'

'No, thank you terribly.'

He poured a full glass for himself as he passed his own place.

'Joanna?'

'No, thanks.'

'Mother?'

'No, no . . . thank you.'

'Tony?'

'Please.'

'Brian?'

'Well . . . yes, all right I'll have a glass.' After all, they'd already had cocktails before dinner and that was enough to make the Old Man turn over in his . . . turn over . . . so what was a glass of port more or less? Besides, it looked excellent. They sipped slowly.

Then more quickly.

Then they gulped it down.

Father could not be ignored. He would not leave them alone to enjoy his port.

'Shall we go?' Mrs Winthorpe caught the eye of Elizabeth, Joanna and Laurine in turn. She stood up and started forward immediately. There should be no detaining her this time. 'You men can stay here and finish your port if you want. . . .'

'We'll all come.' Jack tipped the remaining drops of his port down his throat.

Harry picked up the decanter and put it back in the sideboard, carefully locking the door and putting the key in his pocket.

Brian and Tony made for the door to open it. Both of them walked quickly so as to be there first; at the same time they both tried to look as though they were not having a race. Brian won.

As soon as he heard the door open, Nebuchadnezzar came out from under the sideboard where he had been sitting.

With his tail twitching from side to side he stalked the length of the dining room. He waited at the door while Mrs Winthorpe passed through, followed by Laurine and Elizabeth, who argued playfully in the doorway: 'You first' 'No, you' 'It's your turn' 'Do' until Father bellowed at them: 'Get on. Get on,' and they hurried through the doorway both at once. Joanna followed quickly – was that the tap of a stick behind her?

'Extraordinary how that cat always waited for the Old Boy so that they could walk out side by side,' Harry remarked to Tony.

The big cat went through the doorway, so close to one side that he rubbed against the door jamb as he passed.

He set off down the passage to the drawing room, still keeping well over to the side, leaving plenty of room down the middle.

And down the middle walked Father.

There he was, in his worn velvet smoking jacket, plum-coloured, his thick white hair gleaming in the dim light, shrugging his shoulders now and again as he went slowly along, leaning heavily sideways on his stick.

THE THIRD DAY

I

Brian opened his eyes, grunted, and rolled over to put his arm across the small gap which divided the twin beds. What a nuisance that Jack and Laurine had the only double bed in the whole house. However close one pushed these two damned things there was always a gap.

He found Elizabeth and grunted again with satisfaction. He pressed his cheek deeper into the pillow and closed his eyes to wait for the early morning tea.

Small thoughts ventured into his mind but he was too sleepy to pursue them and they wandered off unattended: the funeral today at eleven . . . Daimler hire . . . Joanna and Andrew, was it? . . . reading the will today. . . .

Reading the will today!

He kept his eye on that one and followed it down to the drawing room where the family gathered in a circle round Mr Trent, who opened the will and started to read: 'This is the last will and testament of . . .'

Should he just hop over the gap into the next bed? He

hated single beds – they both did. Or was he too sleepy? No, he didn't think he was too sleepy – it wasn't far. He pushed back the bedclothes and started to burrow under the clothes of the next bed. Then he stopped, half-immersed, and listened. Was that the rattle of teacups? Footsteps?

Yes! He withdrew hastily and bundled himself back into his own bed. Just in time, he said to himself proudly, as he hoisted the bedclothes up over his shoulders. He shut his eyes tightly and breathed slowly and deeply. The footsteps were outside the door now. . . .

They went past.

Blast! It was not their tea at all. Mother's, probably. His thirst had been thoroughly aroused by the chink of china; now he'd have to wait while Upjohn went all the way downstairs and up again. Even then, it occurred to him, she might do the job in date order, and until Jack and Laurine, and Harry, had been served he'd have to wait.

He lay listening for the footsteps to return a second time, and again they passed his door and continued along the corridor. He'd been quite right. She was doing it in date order. Harry's turn would be next.

Ah. His turn at last. He heard the welcome footsteps halt outside his door, the knock sounded, and passing his tongue lightly over his lips he responded gratefully: 'Come in.'

II

As she was dressing, Laurine remarked to Jack: 'I think I'll wear the diamond brooch this morning.'

'Oh?' said Jack. 'Will you?' It was very large. Very brilliant.

'It's beautiful, and I've had so few chances to wear it since Mother gave it to us.' She paused, hoping that Jack, too, would see her vision of the dinners and dances and theatres to which they had not been.

Jack said nothing.

Laurine realised that he had heard quite well – and under-stood – but was not going to make any comment. It was not pleasant when people ignored remarks, and she went on: 'It was sweet of your mother to give it to you for me.'

'Yes, it was. But, of course, that brooch is an heirloom. The sort of thing that is handed down from generation to generation. . . .' He watched Laurine lift the glittering star of diamonds out of its black velvet case.

Laurine looked up quickly. 'Should I hand it down to my children, then?'

Too late, Jack realised his mistake. 'Oh, well . . . I mean, darling . . . well, we haven't any. . . .'

'Then what will happen to it?'

'I don't know,' he said abruptly. 'Come along! We ought to go and say good morning to Mother. The gong will be going any minute now and we must be down punctually this morn-ing. There's a lot to see to, and I can't leave things to Harry and Brian.'

After all, he told himself as he started out of the room, I am the eldest son. I have responsibilities.

Laurine watched him go, wistfully. He needn't have run off like that. She wasn't going to try to persuade him any more about a baby. . . .

She turned back to the mirror, and held the brooch up against her black dress (*two* new dresses, Jack had given her: one grey, one black). Or should she wear it in her hat? She held it up over her forehead and saw the glitter reflected in her eyes. She put it back in its case, very carefully.

As she hurried along the corridor after Jack, she decided that she would ask Mother which would be the best place to wear the brooch. After all, it had been her brooch. And her taste was faultless.

But Mrs Winthorpe replied doubtfully to Laurine's eager enquiry: 'Well, I don't know . . . would you wear it at all, today? Isn't it a little – large? For a funeral?'

'Do you mean not – not wear it at all?' said Laurine, in so incredulous and grief-stricken a voice that Mrs Winthorpe relented and replied, although still a little uncertainly: 'Well . . . perhaps it might be all right. . . .'

Laurine's face and voice brightened at once.

'In the hat or on the dress?' she enquired enthusiastically.

'Well . . .' It would look equally unsuitable for today in either place. Oh, dear. And in the front pew, too.

'Hat?' suggested Laurine, head on one side, considering her own image in a black velvet hat with a diamond star on it.

'Why not try it after breakfast and see?' suggested Mrs Winthorpe. 'Then you could ask Joanna and Elizabeth what they think.'

Laurine went happily out of the room, still looking at herself wearing the brooch. And today there would be lots more people to look at it. . . .

'No,' Mrs Winthorpe said aloud, when she was alone again. 'There's no need at all to leave her the pearls. . . .'

She stopped quickly as the door opened. Had there been a knock? She hadn't heard it. . . .

'Were you talking to yourself again, Granny?' said Joanna, laughing, as she came into the room followed by Tony. She kissed her grandmother and sat down on the end of the bed.

'No. Well . . . not really. . . .' Mrs Winthorpe felt a little embarrassed. Joanna always seemed to catch her out talking to herself and then she'd tease her about it (she wouldn't like Tony to think she was going, well, queer!). Just as she teased her about never knowing where she had left her spectacles, or under which cushion she had hidden those pieces of jewellery which she didn't bother to lock up in the safe. . . .

'Laurine wants to wear that diamond brooch today. You know, the one Grandfather gave me when Uncle Jack was born which I gave Uncle Jack at the same time I gave you each a piece of the jewellery I never wear. It seemed such a waste to have it lying around,' she said again (as she had said at the time) and repeated: 'Grandfather didn't mind.' Because Alfred used to be rather queer if she gave away his presents, even the ones she no longer used. And sometimes she forgot exactly which ones were his presents. He'd given her such a lot of jewellery.

'Oh, my God!' said Joanna, having recalled and visualised the brooch. 'What a thing to wear for a funeral!'

'I know . . . but . . . well, I did try to point that out, but she seemed so disappointed when I suggested . . . perhaps you could say something? I told her to ask you and Elizabeth. She's not sure whether to wear it at her neck or on her head.'

'Why not on her fanny?' Tony said to Joanna in an undertone.

Joanna jerked to her feet.

'I'm going down to breakfast, Granny. For goodness' sake let Laurine do as she pleases. If she wants to look a sight, surely that's *her* business!'

Mrs Winthorpe watched her go in dismay. What on earth had made her so impatient all of a sudden? Such an edge to her voice. And the way she had looked at Tony.

She smiled at him sadly as he followed Joanna out of the room.

Outside the door he said: 'What's the hurry, sweet?'

She started to walk along the corridor without answering him.

'You know,' he said, closing up to her, 'you're getting awfully careless, sweet. You left the hot tap running in the bathroom this morning. Think of the waste of all that hot water!'

'Did I? Oh dear, I . . . I must have been thinking of . . .' How like Granny I sound, she thought suddenly. She stopped talking, trying to compose herself. What had she been thinking of? When did she leave the tap running? She stopped walking and he stopped too as she swung round to face him. '*Which* tap?' she said.

'The *hot* tap. I *told* you, sweet – don't you listen?'

'In our bathroom?'

'Yes, of course. I heard it running as I came along the corridor, and turned it off. You had your bath after me, you know, so it must have been you.'

'Except that I didn't have a bath in our bathroom. I went to the one by Jack and Laurine's room. It was empty and it was the one I always used when I lived here. So if the hot tap was running, only one person could have left it running. And that's you!'

She watched the pale eyes swivel away from her and a dark flush spread over his face. He's already getting jowly, she thought. In a year or two he'll be gross. For the first time she felt pleasure in the feeling that he was repulsive to her, and she waited for his reply with an excitement tinged with fear, like the excitement of watching a snake that was about to be killed.

He smoothed the trapped anger from his face and said: 'Well, there you are, you see. I hope you're satisfied. You've even got me into your slapdash ways now.'

She stared at him. Surely he must be joking – even if it was only a reversion to one of the little jokes of the old days? She searched for a hint of a rueful smile, and looked at him for so long that he finally grew restive and said, scowling: 'What's the matter?'

She burst out laughing then. It was suddenly as if for years she had been mistaking a clown for a serious actor. Seeing life as a tragedy when really it was a slapstick comedy. Yes! That was it! Slapstick! A clown! How in the world could one be frightened of a clown?

'What's so funny?'

She went on laughing without bothering to answer him. Her laughter was doing her good inside – oh, Lord! It was doing her good!

'Thank goodness she's laughing now!' Mrs Winthorpe exclaimed out loud, as Joanna's peals of laughter reached her. When the laughter finally died away she sank back into her pillows, contented. It was dreadfully worrying when Joanna was snappy with Tony. He was so sweet-tempered himself. She had never, no never once, seen him cross.

Ah! There was the quick, light step of Elizabeth – so gentle and sweet. So soothing after Joanna.

'Hello, Mother. How do you feel this morning?'

And so thoughtful. But how *did* she feel? 'All right, thank you. It's all rather an ordeal, of course. But it must be faced.' She smiled bravely.

'Poor Mother!'

Mrs Winthorpe began to feel much better and she kissed Brian quite cheerfully. Then she began to explain to Elizabeth all about Laurine wanting to wear that unsuitable brooch to the funeral.

'I absolutely agree,' said Elizabeth earnestly. 'It's terribly unsuitable. Shall I just tactfully mention it to her?'

'Would you?' said Mrs Winthorpe, gratefully.

'Yes, of course. I will indeed. Don't you agree, darling?'

'Agree with what?' said Brian.

'You know that enormous diamond brooch Mother gave Jack? Well, Laurine wants to wear it today. On her hat.'

'Or her dress,' Mrs Winthorpe put in.

'And Mother thinks, and I do absolutely agree, that it's really not suitable.'

'Oh, yes. H'm,' said Brian. Really! What trivial things women bothered about! There were important arrangements afoot. If Laurine wanted to wear the bloody thing, let her.

'I think perhaps we ought to go down to breakfast,' he suggested. He wanted to run over the arrangements again and make quite sure that Jack and Harry hadn't made a balls of anything.

'I'll certainly have a word with Laurine,' Elizabeth promised, smiling reassuringly over her shoulder at Mrs Winthorpe as she went out of the room.

'I really don't think she ought to wear it. On her hat at any rate. Do you, darling?' said Elizabeth as she and Brian went downstairs.

'No,' said Brian uninterestedly. 'Perhaps not. . . .' What did it matter *where* she wore the bloody thing! For all he cared she could wear it on her . . .

'I'll just say something tactfully.'

'Yes, do, darling,' he said, hiding his impatience at being interrupted in his thoughts of today's proceedings.

They reached the foot of the stairs, and in his mind Brian arrived with the funeral procession at the church . . . the church . . . the church!

'The church!' he said as he entered the dining room. 'Is somebody in charge of the church?' He nodded brisk greetings all round and swiftly made his way through the smell of kippers to the sideboard.

Tony looked up, wondering if there was an opportunity here to show willingness to help.

Jack looked up, grudgingly because eating a kipper demanded the fullest attention. Harry was not yet down, so Jack took up Brian's challenge: 'In charge?'

'Yes. Flower decorations, and so on.'

'Oh, Miss March is doing all that. She offered to. Very kind

of her. I think she must have had some sort of crush on the Old Boy!' Jack returned to his kipper. 'God knows why,' he added, with his mouth full.

How unkind, Brian thought. Especially as Father was still – he glanced at the clock – for another couple of hours or so, at any rate, available.

'Well, surely,' he pursued, as he returned to the table with cornflakes and coffee, 'some member of the family ought to go to the church this morning?' He sat down firmly in his chair and shook out his table napkin, waiting for someone to offer to go to the church.

Jack said: 'You'd better talk to Mother. She arranged with Miss March about the flower decorations.'

There was silence for a few moments during which Brian could be heard efficiently munching his cornflakes.

'Yes, well . . .' he said at last. 'I think it would, shall we say, *look* better if someone went along and showed a little interest.'

'I'll go,' Joanna offered. The musty smell of that dark old church! And the musty smell of Miss March! But there would also be the sweetness of Madonna lilies and yellow roses, shining out of the darkness.

'I'll come too,' said Laurine. It would give her a chance to get Joanna's support for wearing the brooch today.

'I'll take our car,' said Joanna, and was immediately surprised that she had not asked Tony's permission first. She thought of the tap, streaming out hot water, and laughed again to herself. She glanced at Tony to see if he had noticed anything, but his face gave away nothing.

She swallowed the last of her coffee. 'I don't want any kippers,' she said. 'I'll go and get the car. Laurine, I think we ought to go as soon as you can get ready. Time's getting short.'

III

Miss March almost ran down the aisle towards Joanna and Laurine. Her hair escaped in wisps from beneath her hat. She was in great distress.

'Look!' she wailed, pointing to the black and white mosaic of the aisle. 'Look! They had a special service here for the Boy Scouts last night, and there hasn't been time to get the church properly cleaned yet!'

Joanna and Laurine looked at the muddy footprints on the floor.

'If it hadn't been for that shower of rain we had last evening, it wouldn't have mattered, but look at it! I tried to get one of the women from the cottages across the road to scrub, but do you think they would? They won't do a thing nowadays! It's a disgrace.'

Miss March pulled at her hat in a vain effort to set it straight, but only succeeded in sending it further off course. 'We can't let the Colonel go on his last journey like this!' She was almost in tears.

'We won't!' said Joanna. She surrealised a picture of the luggage lift with its contraption of ropes and chains and pulleys, the bare wooden backstairs, a light green van and an endless mosaic aisle covered with muddy footprints. 'We can

get hold of some water from the cottages, and scrubbing brushes and cloths, then Laurine and I can do it.'

'Yes, yes, that's a good idea!' said Miss March. 'I would help you, gladly, only my knees now . . .'

'No, of course, you mustn't scrub!' said Joanna. 'Don't worry, Laurine and I . . .'

'I'll go and get the things from the cottages.' Laurine hurried off.

'How beautifully you've done the flowers, Miss March!' Joanna said.

'I wanted to be sure it would look nice. For *him*.'

They stood side by side, looking round the dim old church: at the roses and lilies, pale against the dark stone, touched here and there by a rich glow of colour where the sun streamed through the blue or red robe or golden halo of a saint in the stained glass windows. Through the smell of dust and old books and cold damp stone stole the faint, sweet smell of the lilies.

'All the prayer books and the hassocks have got to be put out,' Miss March began to fluster again. 'And I haven't finished the flowers yet. And then there's all the clearing up to do. There's only just over an hour before. . . .'

'I'll put out the books and the hassocks.'

'Oh, would you, dear? Thank you so much. A hymn book, a psalter and a hassock to each person, five persons to the pew.' She hurried back to finish decorating the carved stone font.

Joanna took an armful of dusty green hymn books and grey psalters and set off round the pews. Several times a detached page floated out of one of the books, drifting downwards like a dying butterfly; with difficulty she caught it between her fingers and put it quickly back into the book without stopping to see if it was in its proper place. There was so little time. Soon, now, the bell would begin to toll. . . .

Laurine came back with two large buckets of steaming water, a scrubbing brush and grey cloth floating in each of them.

Joanna seized one of the buckets and went to the top of the aisle, saying to Laurine: 'I'll start at this end, you start at the other, and we'll meet in the middle.'

They scrubbed purposefully and quickly and in silence, watching with pleasure the footprints vanish and the mosaic shine clean through the glaze of water.

As they came face to face, kneeling, in the centre of the aisle, Laurine said: 'Do you think it's all right for me to wear that diamond brooch Mother gave Jack? Today, I mean?'

'Well . . . I wouldn't. But please yourself.'

'You wouldn't?' Laurine paused with the cloth held over her bucket. 'I was going to wear it on the front of my little black velvet cap. It's such a plain little cap, but it's my only black one, and I thought it needed something . . .'

Joanna sat back on her heels. 'Well, I don't think it needs that!' She began to smile. 'If you wear it there, it'll look like one of those things a doctor wears on his forehead when he looks at your tonsils.'

'Will it?' Laurine didn't want to be laughed at. On the other hand . . . 'I tried it on after breakfast, and I thought it looked ever so nice.'

'Well, please yourself. . . .' After all, she thought, it was Laurine's brooch. Why the hell shouldn't she wear it if she wanted to – and where she wanted to. Joanna had a sudden memory of herself throwing away a perfectly good hat, just because Tony objected to it. Hot water tap, indeed! What a fool! She wrung the cloth hard out over the bucket. 'I'll take these things back, and then we'd better go home and get ready as quickly as we can.'

Soon the bell would begin to toll.

Joanna looked up as she crossed the sunlit churchyard. Almost she could see the big bell swinging; hear it . . .

IV

Tony looked at his watch and his lips pressed together until they were a thin line. There was only fifteen minutes to go before the procession started, and Joanna was not back yet. What the hell was she doing?

Jack came down the stairs two at a time. He felt very sprightly in his morning coat, which fitted him perfectly, even though it was thirty years old. Not like Harry's, which was stretched almost to bursting point.

As he went through the hall he noticed Tony standing at the front door like a watchdog. He looked in a hell of a bad mood, Jack thought. He didn't remember ever seeing him look so cross. He moved on towards the drawing room as Joanna's car came up the drive.

'You've been a long time,' Tony said to Joanna as she came through the front door.

Joanna said nothing, and resisted the temptation to give the stuffed grizzly bear a playful dig in the stomach as she went past.

'Did you see anyone you knew?' Tony's glance probed at Laurine.

'We had to help Miss March clean up the church. There'd been a Boy Scout Service last night and the aisle was all muddy, we had to scrub it. Look! I've laddered a new pair of stockings!' Laurine lifted her skirt higher than was necessary but this time Tony never gave her a glance. He was staring after Joanna, who had walked straight past him without a word.

She is impossible, Tony told himself. Impossible.

The sound of cars reached him, and he turned to see three Daimlers and the hearse coming slowly up the drive.

Jack returned from the drawing room, and came to stand beside Tony at the door.

'Ah,' he said. 'Those look all right, don't they? I'll just go out and have a word with the chaps and make sure they know what to do.' He bustled off.

The pall-bearers descended from the hearse and followed Jack into the library through the French window. In a few minutes they emerged with the coffin on their shoulders and carried it slowly, jerkily, to slide it smoothly into the waiting hearse. The wreaths were piled on top of it and on top of the hearse.

Tony watched. There was a faint sneer on his face.

A typical middle-class funeral, he thought, with all its pomp.

A sudden rustle made him turn sharply. The black form of Mrs Winthorpe was silhouetted against the pale square of the landing window as she came down the stairs. Tony put on a charming smile, and as she drew level with him put his arm round her.

'How nice you look, Grandmama,' he said, with infinite tenderness.

She smiled back at him sadly. 'Do I? I feel rather – well, rather – well, you know how one feels.'

'Yes, of course I do.' He gave her a final, very gentle squeeze before letting her go.

'They've seemed so long, these past days. And still two more . . .'

'Ye-e-es,' he saddened his face to tone with his voice. 'I do understand.'

He has such blue eyes, thought Mrs Winthorpe, diverting her mind from wandering off along the tracks of those endless two days. So kind. Joanna's very lucky.

'We'll take care of you, Grandmama. If there's anything – anything at all – I can do, you must be sure to let me know.'

'Thank you so much . . .' Mrs Winthorpe began gratefully. She was interrupted as Brian came bustling down the stairs with Harry close on his heels.

Tony watched Brian's feet descending briskly and pre-cisely: polished feet, perfectly turned out like the neat black hands of a clock at ten to two. Gentlemanly feet: exasperating feet.

'Everything underway?' Brian cocked an enquiring eye on Tony as he passed.

'Everything seems to be proceeding . . .'

But Brian had swept out of earshot, borne on strong wings of efficiency towards an event no part of which could possibly take place without him.

'. . . according to plan,' Tony finished to Harry as he went by on similar but less swift wings.

'Well, I'll just make sure.' Harry, unconvinced, hurried after Brian.

'Now, where are the girls?' Mrs Winthorpe began to fuss. 'They'll be late.'

Trust Joanna, Tony thought. He wondered whether to go and hurry her.

'Could you . . . do you think it would be all right . . . just to sound the gong?'

Tony nodded at Mrs Winthorpe.

'Only very gently. The merest touch. . . .'

Tony nodded again and picked up the stick. Suddenly he wanted to beat the round of metal, to beat it and beat it with all his strength, urging the sound to bellow outward and upward in ring after ring to bring Joanna running in alarm, in *obedience*.

But he only touched the gong very gently.

A distant door opened upstairs, then another door. Elizabeth and Laurine appeared, hurrying, crying: 'Are we late?' as they ran downstairs.

'It's just on time,' said Mrs Winthorpe.

Time to go. Time to start. On the last journey, the weary long procession.

Harry came back into the house.

'Are we all ready?' he asked. 'I think we ought to start getting into the cars now. There's only about two minutes to go before we're due to start. Matthews is waiting at the door for you and Jack, Mother. Laurine and Elizabeth, you come with me' – they huddled towards him – 'where's Joanna?' He frowned.

Mrs Winthorpe looked at Tony anxiously, and he said: 'I'll . . . oh, here she is.'

Joanna came down the stairs without hurrying.

'I've got my taffeta petticoat on. I hope I don't rustle *too* much?' Mrs Winthorpe whispered to Elizabeth.

'No, no, Mother, of course you don't.'

'I like to rustle a little. It feels more important. But not *too* much – for a funeral.'

'No, Mother, of course not.'

'We were about to get in the cars.' Harry looked obviously at his watch as he spoke to Joanna. 'I was just saying who was going with whom.'

'What a nice hat,' Mrs Winthorpe remarked to Joanna. 'Did you get it specially? For the coronation?' Oh, how dreadful! What on earth had made her say 'coronation'?

'No, Granny, not the coronation!' said Joanna. She felt laughter shaking inside her.

'I meant . . . I meant . . .' began Mrs Winthorpe. What *had* she meant? What *could* have made her say . . .?

'Shall we get on?' enquired Harry, ironic politeness covering his impatience.

'Yes, yes, of course. We must!' said Mrs Winthorpe. 'It's time. . . .'

IT IS TIME.

V

'I am the resurrection and the life, saith the Lord.'

The words, dropped into the solemn and hollow silence of the church, reverberating from stone wall to stone wall, find an echo in the heart of each of those seated faithfully in the family pew, ringing them into affinity with the purple-draped coffin before the altar and the discreet and respectful people behind them, delivering them in a body to resurrection and eternity.

'And whosoever liveth and believeth in me shall never die!'

Confidently the words ring out, exhorting, encouraging, promising; and for a brief space each listener is uplifted to a conviction of his own being, imperishable, everlasting – only to be plunged into the chill insinuation of worms under his skin destroying his body (*his* body!) and even while he is still struggling to preserve his flesh from them, he is plunged yet deeper into the depths of futility:

'We brought nothing into this world and it is certain we carry nothing out. The Lord gave and the Lord taketh away.'

As positively and unconcernedly as he had assured them of immortality, the minister forecasts the inevitable destruction of their mortal flesh, the inevitable loss of all their accumulated treasure. Pleased they are indeed to look forward into Eternity, but prefer to slew their glances swiftly past Death, as one might evade the too close scrutiny of a strange and formidable acquaintance whom, in order to reach the dear friend viewed beyond, one must pass.

Discomforted, they finger uneasily their prayer books or their gloves, and with aimless movements of their feet shuffle into position the shabby hassocks in readiness to kneel when called upon, wishing they might close their ears now that they are being no longer uplifted with promises, but harrowed and driven down to the depths of despair.

'And verily every man living is altogether vanity!'

Joanna thought: Even Grandfather. Even Tony. Altogether vanity.

'For man walketh in a vain shadow, and disquieteth himself in vain: he heapeth up riches and cannot tell who shall gather them.'

The vain shadow of Grandfather, gone now: and of Tony . . . .

'Oh spare me a little, that I may recover my strength: before I go hence and be no more seen.'

Strength was beginning to recover . . . a little . . . oh spare me!

She looked at her grandmother, who had never been able to recover her strength, and now who never would. Her face was full of grief, and Joanna knew the grief was not for what she had lost, but for what she had never had the strength to find.

While the clergyman continued to read the Burial Service in the same unmoved and even tones, Mrs Winthorpe was standing before another yet strangely similar clergyman who in place of a purple stole wore a white one embroidered with gold. Her lips moved slightly as she obediently repeated after him: 'I, Dorcas Mary, take thee, Alfred, to my wedded husband, to have and to hold from this day forward . . . for better for worse . . . (oh, surely, surely it has been for worse?) . . . for richer for poorer . . . in sickness and in health . . . to love, cherish and to obey (I tried, Alfred, I tried!) . . . till death us do part. . . .'

Till death us do part!

More than fifty years until Death had come. And although at times those years had seemed endless – an eternity of years – today it seemed but yesterday that she had stood before the altar clothed in white and earnestly spoke the marriage vows from the gracious shelter of her mother's veil.

'For a thousand years in thy sight are but as yesterday: seeing that is past as a watch in the night.'

The lovely words opened her ears and led her along with them gently.

'As soon as thou scatterest them, they are even as a sleep, and fade away suddenly like the grass . . .'

. . . grass at midnight, wet and delicious with falling dew. A night of dancing in a faraway garden. Fairy lights glimmered rare as jewels among the trees. From the nearby lake came the gentle splash of paddles propelling over the calm moonlit surface of the water the slender canoes with Japanese lanterns nodding above their pointed prows like golden oranges.

'We bring our years to an end, as it were a tale that is told.'

An orchestra played among the trees; fans fluttered in the half-light near the lawn. She and Alfred waltzed. The coloured lights, the golden lanterns, the silver-white stars and the pale moon went spinning round and round as, clasped in Alfred's

arms, she turned and swayed and turned again to the lilt of the music.

Her locket, a golden heart on a golden chain, became entangled in his coat.

'I have caught your heart!' he said.

Then: 'Is that true?'

He bent over her, leaning closer his ear to catch, before it was carried away on a breath of air, the faint echo of her whispered yes.

Dutifully she repeated Mr Russell's 'Amen.'

She watched him leave his place to go to the lectern, watched his familiar pause and half-turn reverence altarwards, outswirling cassock revealing a sturdy and well-polished boot; she watched him gently and absent-mindedly draw through his fingers the purple embroidered bookmark in the great book open on the lectern, adjust his spectacles, raise his eyebrows. She heard him clear his throat and begin to read: 'Now Christ is risen from the dead, and become the first fruits of them that slept. For since by man came death . . .'

'First fruits and enemies' – dusky peaches, purple-bloomed plums, grapes, red apples glowed and enemies glowered at her – but the words gave her no lead and she could follow no further.

Alfred came back, produced for her impromptu his performance in 'Mrs Jarley's Waxworks'. She could see the title on a hand-painted banner strung across the home-made stage between the blue velvet drawing room curtains looped back by Eva and Carrie and allowed to fall together again at the close of each scene. It was the amateur theatrical party which Alfred's mother had given for them to celebrate their engagement.

All the performers were supposed to be waxworks. They had to be wound up by Mrs Jarley (played by Alfred's mother) before they were able to move or speak. Then they jerked their limbs in stilted gestures, and spoke in jerky, falsetto voices.

Strange, she could not remember the scenes; not even the ones in which she herself had played – what they were supposed to represent, what happened in them even. She could remember only one thing; Alfred, wound up and set off by Mrs Jarley, pointing automatically with vigorous, consecutive movements of his right arm and repeating: 'Big Box! Little Box! Band Box! Bundle!'

Each word, clearly and separately articulated, burst from beneath his moustache like a miniature explosion.

What did it mean?

He must have been going on a journey, with his boxes. Where? Why?

Like a gramophone record, falsified, mechanical: 'Big Box! Little Box! Band Box! Bundle!' Emphasised by the same pointlessly forceful gestures of the right arm, the voice repeated over and over, as if the needle had caught on a flaw in the record: 'Big Box! Little Box! Band Box! Bundle!'

Where was he going? Why was he going? Who was going with him? Not she: for she was watching from the wings.

She could see the mechanism beginning to run down. The gestures became slower and less forceful, the words slurred and drawled:

'Big Box . . . Little . . . Box . . . Band . . . Box . . . Bun-n-n-d-le. . . .'

The movements grew slower and slower, the pauses between the words longer while, powerless herself to give them further impetus, she waited for them to cease altogether.

The arm lifted, descended once more in meek obedience to the impulse, and returned to immobility; the weary voice pronounced finally 'Big Box . . .' and was silent.

'O death, where is thy sting? O grave, where is thy victory?' These were words she knew! These were words which led her out of the valley of the past and guided her feet along a way not altogether fearful – perhaps death would have no sting, the grave no victory. Death was swallowed up in victory!

She pondered the words of the clergyman as he spoke, and in accordance with them felt steadfast, immovable. She believed. Her labour would not be in vain!

Comforted and grateful, she joined with the rest of the congregation in the Lord's Prayer.

She saw the purple-draped coffin hoisted smoothly onto the shoulders of the waiting men. She watched it pass her at the start of its journey through the church, borne up higher than the heads of the people. It seemed to have very little to do with Alfred.

Holding Jack's arm, she followed the coffin on its unhurried journey out of the church, keeping her eyes fixed firmly upon it but conscious also of the dark figures stretching away, rank upon rank, on either side of her, with unidentified faces like pale and curious masks closely watching her as she passed.

VI

Down the aisle and out between the carved doors of the church they flowed, two and three deep in a dark river which broke outside the porch into separate streams proceeding quietly and unobtrusively each along its own particular course or, checked by the restraining influence of chance-met acquaintances, converging into pools of low-toned discussion.

Mrs Winthorpe looked round anxiously. She tried to sort out the more important of the people eddying about her in the lane, those to whom she must speak, old friends whose feelings must not be hurt. The men replacing their top hats and the women pulling on their gloves as they came out of the church seemed to have lost their identity in their mourning, and it was difficult to distinguish among them those to whose words of comfort she must listen, speak in return a few words of acknowledgement and admit them, with small scraps of information concerning Alfred's last hours, into the intimacy to which, over the long years of the past, they had gained right of entry.

A tall man detached himself from the crowd and walked towards her raising his hat. Who? There was something about him which she recognised – but his face was unfamiliar. In the few seconds' grace while he was drawing near she searched desperately in her memory for a name, trying to use for guide the almost-known light of his eyes. But it was like looking into the windows of a strange house at a friend overshadowed and made unrecognisable by the altered surroundings.

The man spoke. She was shocked into recognition. Charlie! She ought to have remembered him – their best man! She hoped he had not noticed her hesitation. How he had altered! Well, of course. He must be nearly Alfred's age and she had not seen him for more than thirty – perhaps forty – years. Ever since he had once (in front of everyone, too, quite openly) picked a rose and handed it to her, and Alfred said it had a hidden meaning and poor Charlie was never asked to the house again. But how good of him to come to Alfred's funeral.

She wondered if he thought she had altered a great deal. *He* looked terribly aged. She talked to him, saying how good it was of him to come all this way (did he still live in the same place?) after all these years, and what a pity they had lost touch. They must not lose touch again, she said, knowing as she spoke that there was no longer any point of contact between them. As she talked to him, she thought how sad it was that one must lose, one after another, the friends of one's youth. Until today, she realised, she had thought of Charlie (if she thought of him at all) as a tall, strong, self-assured, good-looking young man (so scrupulously clean that one could almost smell the soap on his fair freckled skin) with golden hair and laughing blue eyes. Now that young man was dead, quite killed by Charlie himself; and with him died another part of her youth. The empty place was taken by this unsteady stranger, with white hair, withered skin the colour of a candle, and tired eyes that held only the faintest echo of long-silent laughter.

It was a relief when at last he turned away and other people came to speak to her, people with whom she had been

constantly in touch, and whom she had been able to watch being altered by time with no sense of shock.

She acknowledged sympathy, answered questions, nodded and bowed this way and that, while her eyes went roving over the crowd to make sure her attention missed no one who was trying, even humbly and without certainty of success, to attract it. Throughout, her mind was busy selecting those whom she ought to invite for lunch – those who were related, those who had come from a long way off.

'Do stay for lunch!' she begged Enid and John Bradley, hoping they would refuse. They accepted. She resigned herself. They had come a long way; they were old friends.

Charlie! She must ask him to lunch. He was such an old friend, and he had come such a long way. She raised her chin to look for him above the crowd, but he was nowhere to be seen. She felt a brief pang of guilt. She ought to have asked him. But it was too late now. She turned back to the few remaining people. Only a very thin trickle was coming out of the church now, one or two of the tradespeople with whom they had dealt for years; the family servants, the Browns, the Liptons, Jordan, Upjohn. . . .

'Mother, I think we ought to be getting back for lunch.' Jack touched her arm.

Mrs Winthorpe smiled at him. How helpful he was, talking to people: she had noticed him, while she had been engaged with Charlie, being charming to everyone.

'I think we ought to be getting back for lunch,' he repeated.

'Yes . . .' Her forehead wrinkled. She was being swept along now by a great wave over which she could not lift her head to see the land, which all but engulfed her; a wave which seemed to flow so swiftly yet took so long to reach anywhere, carrying her on and on, without a break, endlessly.

'Goodbye, goodbye!' she said to the Robinsons. They did not live far away; there was no need to ask them to lunch. What a pity about Charlie . . .

Her eyes roved once again over the few remaining people . . . all local, thank goodness. The ham was not very large, and she had only ordered two chickens. They would already be – let's see – their eight selves and Mr Russell, that made nine, Eva and Carrie, eleven, and – good heavens! – John and Enid, that made thirteen.

She counted once more, on her fingers, to make quite certain. They couldn't possibly sit down thirteen! She must speak to Harry, to Jack, to somebody. . . . She searched desperately through the few people still left. They were nearly all local people; she could hardly ask one of them because the others would wonder why they hadn't been invited as well, and that would never do.

Oh, there was Cousin Laura! But she was such a queer old thing. Still, they couldn't sit down thirteen. She started to walk towards Cousin Laura.

Then she saw Mary Leigh talking to Harry. What a relief! And how stupid of her not to have remembered. Of course, she had already asked Harry to invite Mary for lunch. That made fourteen. Dear Mary! What a pity Harry and Mary didn't . . . she would have approved of Mary Leigh as a daughter-in-law (and one knew something about her family too, which was so nice).

As she made her way on Jack's arm to the Rolls she smiled warmly at Mary.

Brian caught them up and said in an undertone: 'Mother, I've asked Cousin Laura to lunch. The poor old thing's come a long way, and she looks as if she could do with a decent meal. Is that all right?'

There was a slight pause, then Mrs Winthorpe said: 'Yes, yes, quite all right, of course.'

How irritating! There was no need to ask Cousin Laura to lunch. They were already fourteen. And that was quite enough for a small ham and two chickens (it was only a quick, *light* luncheon). Besides, Cousin Laura was such a queer old thing. That red hair – dyed, of course – and the way she sometimes took more than was good for her (fortunately, today there would only be sherry handed round by Upjohn who knew all about Cousin Laura). All the same she wished Brian hadn't . . . and without asking her first. . . . Besides, she sent Cousin Laura twenty pounds a year and most of her old clothes. She looked more closely at Cousin Laura and recognised her own black ostrich feather boa – but how stringy! How bedraggled! That had been a lovely boa once. No, there was no need to ask Cousin Laura to lunch, no need at all.

'I wish you'd just mentioned it to me first,' said Mrs Winthorpe in a loud whisper as Brian turned to join Harry and Laurine and Elizabeth in the second car.

'Sorry, Mother . . .' said Brian.

A small delight rubbed guilty hands and smiled in Jack's mind, just as it used to when they were boys and he was not

the one to be punished; it always made him feel a little bit bigger.

'. . . I thought you'd want to ask her,' Brian explained. 'As she *is* one of the family.'

'Yes, but only second cousin once removed.' Mrs Winthorpe looked again at Cousin Laura, who stood with her toes turned slightly inwards and the feather boa drooping on either side of her thin neck as she waited meekly but expectantly to be beckoned into the family circle.

'Tell her,' Mrs Winthorpe said to Brian, and she smiled very kindly at Cousin Laura, '. . . that there is room for her – in the third car.'

Mrs Winthorpe climbed into the Rolls, Jack settled himself beside her, and Matthews spread across their knees the rug, the thin one, the summer one.

While they waited for the procession to start back along the lane Mrs Winthorpe ran on ahead in her thoughts to the dining room. She hoped there would be enough food; she thought there would be. She sized up the ham, crisply covered with golden breadcrumbs, and the two chickens, dressed in white chaudfroid sauce buttoned with black truffles sitting among curled, tender, pale jades of lettuces. And there would be plenty of little cakes and pastries – from the confectioners, because one never knew (whatever Harry might say) how Mrs Burton's cakes would turn out. There would be sherry beforehand: Rich, Brown, Soft, Fruity! – she had seen the label – although she had not really thought sherry absolutely necessary, at a funeral. Nor had Jack. But Brian, and even Harry, had insisted.

'What about the – the – whatever you call them – the men
...?' She waved her hand towards the hearse. 'And the dri-
vers? They know they're to go into the servant's hall for some
lunch, don't they?'

'Yes,' said Jack. 'I told them.'

What about Alfred? He would wait for them, she supposed,
outside.

He would not have long to wait.

VII

'Have you a soda mint, Mother?' said Brian after lunch, as Mrs
Winthorpe came back into the hall, pink with the exertion of
seeing Mr Russell on his way to the crematorium, saying
goodbye to Eva and Carrie and Mary, and arranging with the
Bradleys to give Cousin Laura a lift to the station.

'Yes, I . . .' Mrs Winthorpe began to rummage through the
contents of her black bag for the little enamel box in which
she kept her mints. 'I thought it was . . . now where?' Her
pinkness deepened. 'Oh, yes. I remember now. I didn't trans-
fer it from my other bag. It's upstairs, I'm afraid. Why?'
Sympathy and eagerness to help animated her voice. 'Have
you got indigestion?'

'Yes,' said Brian sadly. 'I have indeed.'

There was a small silence into which Mrs Winthorpe's 'Oh,
dear' floated as gently as a feather and was lightly blown away
by the airy indifference of the others.

Harry looked at his watch. 'You've had three-quarters of an
hour!' he pronounced, and the last word, broken into three

syllables, up-down-up, sounded like the notes of a-a-men on the organ. 'And,' he went on, 'we should have started ten minutes ago, according to my schedule. We shall be late!'

'I can't help that!' Brian started towards the staircase. 'It's not *my* fault that I've got indigestion. I must take a soda mint before I go.'

'. . . in my blue bag in the top left-hand drawer of my dressing table,' put in Mrs Winthorpe.

'And as for being late, we were hanging about outside the church for goodness knows how long,' Brian said plaintively over his shoulder.

'Oh, but, darling, we had to talk to old friends!' Mrs Winthorpe protested after him. '. . . in the top left-hand drawer, remember!'

'Mother, shall you and I go and get in the car?' suggested Jack, seeing Harry's frown which became deeper as he waited for Brian to reappear; he squeezed Laurine's hand: 'Goodbye, darling! See you presently!' He took his mother's arm and led her outside.

'Brian will be down in two ticks,' Elizabeth said, to pacify Harry. 'Shall we start getting in the car?' She looked at Laurine, and noticed for the first time that she was not wearing the brooch. Perhaps no one would have noticed if she *had* worn it, poor little thing!

'Yes, you'd better get in,' said Harry, and with a last impatient glance up the stairs he followed them out to the second car.

Brian came bustling up to overtake them in the courtyard and jump briskly into the waiting car. He felt much better. He had one soda mint in his mouth and another in his pocket.

As Tony sat down beside her in the third car Joanna looked out of the back window and realised that they were the last car in the procession now because no relatives or staff were going to the crematorium, only the immediate family.

She turned back to look at the two cars in front. Over the tops of them she could see the flowers which crowned the hearse quiver into movement and slowly draw away. Then the first car started to move, followed by the second, and lastly the one in which she and Tony were sitting. Smoothly, sedately, they proceeded out of the courtyard between the wrought-iron gates, down the avenue of elms, past the stone shrine, out onto the main road, still at the same slow, stately pace.

Joanna said after a few minutes: 'We're not going to get there in time. We ought to be there in half an hour, but at this rate it'll take us an hour at least.'

'Yes. Perhaps we're going to be late.'

'But what will happen?'

'We'll have to wait and see, won't we?' There was that familiar, faint jeer in his voice, designed to make her feel she had said something silly. This time she did not feel, as she had so often felt in the past, embarrassed and unhappy. She simply didn't care.

She went on: 'But I heard Uncle Harry say we must be punctual at the crematorium whatever happened, because they always had so many to . . . to do.'

Would he miss his turn? A conveyor belt of coffins stretched before her, each coffin waiting its turn to be tipped, narrow end foremost, into the fiery furnace.

'Then they'll have to speed up the production line, won't they?' Still the faint jeer. He jerked up his sleeve and looked at his watch. As if in response to his unspoken demand, the car began to accelerate.

'We're beginning to pick up a bit now.'

'Uncle Brian will be shocked if we go too fast,' Joanna remarked, leaning forward for a better look at the car ahead. She could see through the back window the outline of four heads, swaying and jolting. . . .

'Aren't we going a little fast?' said Brian, as he felt himself being hustled along at ever-increasing speed.

'The driver of the hearse has his orders,' Harry replied shortly. 'He knows what time the service is to take place, and he will naturally do his best to be there by that time.'

'Within the bounds of decency, I hope!'

Harry said nothing.

Brian went on. 'As you know, Mother is nervous of being driven too fast at the best of times. This, above all, is hardly the time she should be subjected to it.'

'There's nothing we can do about it. There's no way we can slow them down. One can hardly hoot one's horn in a funeral procession.'

'Hardly!' Brian paused for a moment, then continued: 'But I still think it was a pity the cremation was not arranged for three o'clock instead of half-past-two. That extra half-hour would have made all the difference!' He felt in his pocket for the other soda mint, and could not resist adding: 'I told you so at the time.'

Harry compressed his lips, saying to himself that he was

not going to be drawn into an argument whilst he was taking part in a funeral procession – Father's funeral procession too – but suddenly his mind changed. Brian – funeral procession or no – must not be allowed to get away with saying: 'I told you so' to *him*! He said: 'If you think you could have done it so much better than anyone else, you should have made the arrangements yourself.'

'I was scarcely given the chance, was I?' Brian's voice clamped round Harry quite gently but with steel.

A tiny sound of laughter escaped Laurine which she quickly changed to a cough.

Caught in his own trap, Harry knew he could not fight his way out; but if he refused to budge, sat there fair and square, it would release him of its own accord. 'I am not going to argue with you at a time like this,' he said, circumflexing his eyebrows and pursing his lips.

Elizabeth watched Brian's eyes go blank. He had pulled down the blind of indifference behind which no one could penetrate, no one could have the satisfaction of seeing what he was thinking. If only Mother had been able to protect herself like that, thought Elizabeth – poor Mother, whose large graceful black hat she could see swaying beside Jack's neat head in the first car. . . .

'Aren't we going a little fast?' enquired Mrs Winthorpe nervously. 'I don't like going fast round corners! Besides, for a funeral, it's not . . . oh!' She clutched Jack's arm as they swayed round an extra sharp bend in the road.

He set her upright again and reassured her. 'We're not really going very fast, Mother. It just . . . seems fast.'

'Oh, but we are! We are!' She leaned forward to peer over Matthews' shoulder at the speedometer.

'What does it say?' she asked shakily. 'I can't quite see . . . I haven't got my distance glasses.'

'Thirty-five,' lied Jack. The speedometer needle pointed to almost sixty. Good for old Matthews!

'Oh, thirty-five.' Relieved, Mrs Winthorpe sank back in her seat. A moment later she was upright again. 'Are you *sure*? I feel as if I'm going very much more than thirty-five.'

'No, no, it's quite all right. Thirty-five.' Jack patted her arm.

Ahead of them the hearse flashed out of sight round a corner. They rounded the corner themselves and saw it come into view again, travelling so swiftly, so determinedly, so – so – *pitilessly*, that Mrs Winthorpe would not have been surprised to see all the flowers come sliding off the top of the hearse to fall in a great heap of colour by the wayside.

'I don't suppose,' she said to Jack sadly, 'that Father has ever been as fast as this before in his life!'

As they journeyed over the long road she tried for at least part of the time to look out of the side windows. But always her eyes returned to stare ahead at the hearse, now disappearing, now reappearing, round bend after bend in the road – always a little way ahead of them but not far enough for anything to come between – to watch with almost horror the grey road racing between its wheels like an endless river, to watch anxiously the flowers on top of it, or, through the square of glass at the back, so magnified in comparison with the back window of an ordinary car that it resembled a shop window or a showcase, the pale coffin, on which she looked with pity.

Alfred abhorred speed and it seemed somehow so wrong that he should be made to travel at such a pace, whisking round corners without dignity in spite of the occasional uncovering of heads by a few of the men who watched them pass (not all men, for those good old days of respect and courtesy were gone for ever now). There he was, helpless even to protest: could only lie, enclosed, and be hustled willy-nilly to his own destruction.

They reached the crematorium at one minute past two.

Mr Russell waited for them on the steps of the large white building, the starched folds of his clean surplice blowing in the breeze. He was watching the coffin being carried past him on the shoulders of the four pall-bearers.

Mrs Winthorpe eased herself out of the car onto Jack's waiting arm, and they followed Mr Russell into the crematorium.

Inside, Mrs Winthorpe stopped suddenly. A chill passed through her.

The men had stripped the coffin of its flowers and abandoned it in the centre of a blue-curtained stage at the farthest end of the long, empty building. It looked so small and bare. And so alone.

'Big Box, Little Box . . .' Where was the furnace? Her hand tightened on Jack's arm.

He put his hand over hers and whispered: 'All right, Mother?'

Together they moved forward, slowly.

Behind them, Harry, walking alone, stopped to wipe his feet.

Brian kept out of range of the busy heels and Joanna moved up beside him. Together they waited for Harry to have done.

Joanna thought: Why is Uncle Harry wiping his feet? The sight was ridiculous, humorous; but sadness filled her, casting its shadow upon amusement and extinguishing it. The solid body, the curly grey head, the well-kept hands, the precise and careful feet on the mat performing their drill even in the face of death: all this in less than a hundred – in less than fifty – years would be nothing.

Harry himself – like Grandfather – would be nothing.

They should be clean now, Harry said to himself. He looked over his shoulder to make sure Brian was following, then started off down the aisle.

One by one they moved silently into the two front pews, seated themselves and leaned forward to pray.

'Man that is born of woman has but a short time to live and is full of misery. . . .'

Once more Mr Russell shed his familiarity and became a prophet.

'. . . He cometh up, and is cut down like a flower . . .'

with one sweep of the scythe, the scarlet poppy and the white marguerite

'. . . he fleeth as it were a shadow . . .'

hastening across the light green field the darker green of the shadow

'. . . and never continueth in one stay. In the midst of life we are in death: of whom may we seek for succour. . . .'

Were the blue curtains drawing together? Mrs Winthorpe

stared at them, telling herself that it must be imagination, they could not possibly . . . and yet they were. They were moving. Eva and Carrie. Big Box, Little Box . . .

'. . . earth to earth, ashes to ashes, dust to dust. . . .'

One by one they became conscious of the slow, relentless narrowing of the stage. With every word the space between the curtains grew less.

'Lord, have mercy upon us.'

The curtains encroached silently, minutely, stealthily.

'Christ, have mercy upon us.'

In the diminishing space the coffin seemed to grow larger, threatening the stage.

'Lord, have mercy upon us.'

Nearer, nearer together drew the curtains; the movement of them seemed to close like a giant hand upon all their hearts.

The coffin was enormous now.

Hiding their faces, closing their eyes, they murmured the Lord's Prayer, and swiftly at the amen their eyelids flew up, eager yet fearful to see the coffin still unhidden.

'We give thee hearty thanks for that it hath pleased thee to deliver this our brother out of the miseries of this sinful world . . . .'

The stage was dominated now by the coffin, which had assumed vast proportions.

They wanted to cry out, to arrest the curtains, somehow to delay the last, the final, departure.

But they stood dumb, helpless.

'The grace of our Lord Jesus Christ, and the love of God, and the fellowship of the Holy Ghost, be with us all evermore.'

Through the minute crack now left between the curtains they saw the last of the coffin, the last of that great tapered form which still, although strange and altered, preserved the mould of the man they had known. Although breath had gone, life had gone, the form, the shape, was still there . . . then it too was gone.

'Amen.'

VIII

Upjohn broke into the silence of the drawing room with the loaded tea tray. She saw Mr Jack, Mr Harry and Mr Brian, seated in a row on the sofa, each reading from a large bundle of stiff white papers tied together with green ribbon. Mrs Winthorpe, seated by the window in her faded armchair, was looking on with a worried frown.

As Upjohn laid the tea, with careful hands so expert from habit that they no longer required the co-operation of mind or eyes, she watched them all, discreet and unobserved.

Mr Jack's eyes darted here and there over the black writing on his papers, as he quickly turned over sheet after sheet with one hand and with the thumb and forefinger of the other hand picked at his nose.

Mr Harry pursed his lips and raised his eyebrows, now and then nodding to himself as he went slowly and methodically through the papers. Mr Brian read quietly, his expression unchanged except when his nose twitched sideways in an occasional long, slow, almost silent sniff.

When she was unable to prolong any further the laying of the table, Upjohn gave one last critical look, mentally patting each piece of rose-wreathed china into place. Reluctantly, she picked up the empty tray and, without hurrying, passed behind the sofa on her way to the door. She looked sideways, over the three bent heads, at the white papers. But the print was not large; her eyesight was not good. Besides, she would never have dreamt of reading over anyone's shoulder.

As she went out of the room Miss Joanna, on her way in, nearly collided with her.

'Sorry, Upjohn! Why don't you hoot your horn round corners?'

The very idea! Upjohn said to herself as she went more warily to the back quarters.

Joanna went to sit near her grandmother.

Mrs Winthorpe motioned with her hand towards the three men on the sofa.

'The will.' she said, in a hushed voice.

So they had it already? Joanna looked at the clock and saw that they had been back from the crematorium exactly half an hour.

'Have you seen it?' she asked, noticing that her grandmother's hands were empty.

'No, there were only three copies. I'll see it later. I don't suppose it will make much difference to me now.' She closed her eyes and leant her head against the back of the chair. How lovely it would be to go to sleep. . . .

'Well,' said Harry, injecting satisfaction into the silence. 'I think that's all reasonably clear. A very fair will, I call it.'

'There are one or two things I don't quite get . . .' Jack began. He hesitated, saying to himself again that one thing at least was clear (thank God): he had not been cut out. All that worry for nothing. He got as much during his lifetime as Harry and Brian. But . . .

'After I die . . .' he began again.

'I don't think there's any need to go into that now,' said Harry.

There was a slight pause. Then Jack said: 'Right. Any time. Whenever you like.' But it must be gone into – he must get Laurine's position straight.

He tried very hard to rejoice that he had not been cut out of Father's will. But he could not feel overjoyed. He could not even feel the tremendous relief he had expected to feel.

He tried to imagine how he would have felt had he received no money at all: not a penny. Not a farthing. By contrasting that darkness with the light of obtaining his own fair share, he tried to edge into the light's radiance, to sit down in it and bask a little.

Thank God I get as much as Harry and Brian, he said to himself again, but . . .

Harry! Brian! Not only were they executors when he, the eldest son, was not (that had been bad enough), but they were trustees for *his* money. He had not even been allowed by Father to have control over his own money. He, the eldest son! Besides . . .

'Come along, everybody. Tea.' called Mrs Winthorpe, leaving the soft comfort of her armchair with a sigh. Tea. Such a nuisance. It ought to be done away with.

'You pour out, darling,' she said wearily to Joanna, thinking: if Sylvia had been alive, she would have poured out.

Joanna took Mrs Winthorpe's place behind the silver kettle singing above a blue flame.

Seated at the head of the table, in Father's place, and sadly watching the sandwiches circulate, Jack thought that Harry might as well sit here – might just as well!

Mrs Winthorpe held the plate of sandwiches towards Brian.

Brian stared at it until it took on clearer-cut reality, succeeding the new hard court, the bathing pool, the flower-patterned, yellow-fringed, garden swing-seat he was going to buy; recalling him from the South of France, where he had been sunbathing, swimming, buying pretty girls cool drinks
. . . .

'No, thank you. . . .'

Mrs Winthorpe was disappointed. She had ordered egg sandwiches specially. They were Brian's favourite.

He suddenly spied the delicate yellow diced with white oozing between the thin slices of bread on the plate which was being slowly withdrawn by Mrs Winthorpe's disappointed hand.

'Oh, are they egg?' he cried.

'Yes!' The plate wavered and returned once more.

'Good!' he said happily. 'I'll take two, shall I, as they're so small?'

'You know,' said Harry, 'death duty is going to be very high.'

'It is indeed,' said Brian. He paused to consume in one mouthful his first egg sandwich.

'It might be a good idea,' he went on, surreptitiously wiping his fingers on the crochet edge of the tablecloth, 'to avoid some death duty by each of us taking one or two things from the house before the probate chap comes. Small things,' he added hastily, seeing Jack look up at the chandeliers.

He popped his second sandwich into his mouth.

Harry paused to think carefully before answering.

Yes, he decided at last, that would probably be all right. Father could hardly object to a few things (small things) being taken to avoid death duty. Father had always grumbled about the government anyway (whichever party was in power).

'There are those small things in the cabinet in the library,' he remarked.

'Yes,' said Brian. 'And there are those first editions.'

'We'll have to see about those,' said Harry. 'But the cabinet for a start – immediately after tea, I should think, while we're all here. And later on, Brian, I'd like to have a talk with you, privately.'

Privately? What was on Harry's mind, Brian wondered.

Such queer things in that cabinet, thought Mrs Winthorpe. Whatever could anyone want with them?

Laurine felt a shiver of excitement. The little watch was in that cabinet. She longed to get at it.

'We'll take it in turns to select a piece each, in order of seniority,' said Harry. 'Do you agree, Brian?'

'Yes.'

'Jack goes first . . .'

'What about Mother?' asked Jack.

'Oh, no. No. I've got far too much jewellery already.' She put out her hands to ward off those queer objects, all those beads and bangles which reminded her of naked savage women with dreadful brown elongated bosoms. She shivered.

'Are you cold, Mother?' Elizabeth asked. 'Shall I shut the window?' She saw that the window was not open, and amended hastily: 'Or get you a wrap?'

'No, thank you,' said Mrs Winthorpe, and she went on: 'You all take those things if you want to. I think it would be a very good idea. I can't bear to think of the horrid government taking so much in death duty. Why ever should they?'

'That's settled then!' said Harry, cutting in on Tony, who was just beginning to explain kindly to Mrs Winthorpe all about the economy of Great Britain. 'We'll take it in turns to pick one piece at a time, starting with you, Jack.'

IX

In the centre of the library there was now a bare space, rectangular, with chairs and small tables huddled round the outer edges.

Treading warily, and pressing close to the pushed-back furniture to avoid walking on the bare space, they made their way to the cabinet.

A few frail feathers of fern lay scattered about the carpet, a handful of small round mauve and white petals like confetti
. . . .

Mrs Winthorpe peered into the cabinet. 'I really don't know what you'll find to choose from out of this . . .'

'Well, I know what I'm going to choose,' said Jack. 'That is . . .' he looked round at Harry and Brian '. . . if I'm really to begin?'

'Yes, go ahead.'

Laurine wondered: will he choose the little watch? For me? Her breathing quickened; her cheeks grew warm. In imagination it was already on her lapel; she could hear it ticking away gently below her left ear.

Harry took the master key from Father's key ring – which was in *his* pocket now. He opened the door of the cabinet.

Jack reached in. For a second his hand hovered; then descended. 'This!' he said, and he drew out a small bronze plaque.

What on earth is it, Laurine wondered. She had never even noticed it before. What on earth was Jack . . .?

'Oh!' said Mrs Winthorpe. Happiness rushed into her. She felt all warm and rosy. 'Do you really want that? Father did that of me years and years ago, when we were engaged.'

Laurine could have wept. Why on earth had Jack . . .? And there were three more people to come before it was Jack's turn again! Surely he hadn't forgotten how she loved that watch?

'I love it!' said Jack.

Mrs Winthorpe withdrew to sit in the window seat and bask in the warmth of Jack's thought for her.

'Your turn now, Harry,' Brian prompted.

Harry looked into the cabinet dubiously. There was really not much in it that he wanted. There was that small enamel watch . . . he had half thought of going in for watches . . .

old watches. But this did not look a particularly outstanding specimen anyway.

Laurine, seeing him looking at the watch, held her breath; then sighed with relief as he passed it over and selected a small crystal vase.

'My turn now,' said Brian, popping in his hand and drawing out the watch. He pinned it on Elizabeth's shoulder.

Laurine gazed at it, on *Elizabeth's* shoulder, until it became blurred and her throat felt choked and she had to turn away.

'Oh, darling, how lovely!' said Elizabeth.

'Go on, Joanna,' said Brian. 'It's you now.'

Joanna looked into the cabinet. She wanted the shell, the shell which looked as if it were made of moonlight. But she also wanted a caged ivory parrot being teased by a monkey with a nut. Which should she take? Probably no one else would want the shell so there would be a chance to pick it next time. She took the monkey and parrot.

Laurine looked at Jack with eyes pleading. If she could not have the watch, perhaps she could have the coral necklace? She had so often said in front of him what a pretty necklace it was – surely he would remember? Why was he hesitating?

'Go on,' said Joanna. 'It's your turn again, Uncle Jack.'

'Oh, is it? I say – are you sure this is – I mean, is it all right?'

'We're only avoiding death duty,' Brian pointed out.

Laurine made a sudden movement of impatience, and Jack turned to her: 'Shall I take the belt with the pewter buckle, darling? It looks as if it would just about go round your waist. Would you like it?'

'Yes, please!' After all, the belt was lovely. The necklace could wait till next time round.

Harry took the twin to his crystal vase.

Brian took the little model of a Spanish galleon in silver.

Joanna took a carved ivory fish. She would let the shell go for another round to enjoy the excitement of almost, but not quite, possessing it.

Jack took a paper knife, without consulting Laurine.

Harry took a leather bookmark.

Brian took a soapstone crab.

Joanna took the coral necklace.

It's not fair, thought Laurine. Jack was the eldest, and all the nice things were going to the others. The fairest way would have been if each had made a choice of all the things they wanted at once – starting with the eldest, of course.

Once more Jack stretched out his hand, this time for a bracelet.

One after another they went on dipping into the cabinet, quickly now, without hesitation, without repetition of Jack's initial reluctance.

One by one the objects disappeared: necklaces, earrings, native ornaments, knives, bracelets. . . .

The cabinet was beginning to look bare, plundered.

Joanna examined the carved ivory figure in her hand as she carried it across to her accumulated pile of treasure. Her concentration upon its intricate detail was deflected by a sudden unbeckoned image of red flames leaping at the end of a cold white building. Her hand shook. She shuddered away from the roar and the heat and the smell of burning.

Is it going on now? Now, at this very moment? Or is it all over? Ashes?

'Your turn, Joanna,' Brian nudged her.

'And I think that must be the last,' Harry pronounced. 'The cabinet's practically empty. Besides, it's getting on for dinner time and I want a short discussion with you, Brian, as I said, before we go upstairs. Something has just occurred to me. . . .' He glanced at Joanna.

Joanna felt her hand close at last on the smooth silver shell. She rocked it in her palm as Harry shut the door of the cabinet. He locked it carefully, although it was empty now except for a piece of wood which someone – Father? – had started to carve, some old coins, a cracked vase, a broken necklace, a few stray beads. . . .

X

'We'll light the hall fire this evening,' said Mrs Winthorpe. 'It seems to have turned very chilly.'

She drew the folds of her black velvet housecoat close around her.

'Oh, yes,' she said, entering the hall. 'Far too cold to sit without a fire.'

Nebuchadnezzar trailed past her and jumped to his usual place on the tapestry stool in front of the fireplace.

Mrs Winthorpe went to look at the thermometer which hung from one of the gilt wall brackets.

'It's only sixty!' she said indignantly.

'You pay far too much attention to those things,' Harry

admonished her. 'Just because the thermometer says such and such you feel so and so.'

'No, I don't. I felt cold before I ever looked at it. I said I did.'

'Then why look at it?'

'I . . . I . . . well, I *like* to look at it.'

'You're never happy until you get the room up to seventy. And that's far too hot. I can't stand stuffy rooms. They send me to sleep.'

What nonsense! Brian thought. Harry would go to sleep after a meal regardless of the temperature. Besides, he ought not to speak to Mother like that.

'I don't go entirely by the thermometer,' Mrs Winthorpe went on pleading her case. 'It's not fair to say that I do. I know when I'm warm and I know when I'm cold. And I'm cold now!' She said it quite defiantly, and looked round the waiting group for someone to support her. She appealed to Tony: 'Don't you call it cold tonight?'

'Well, Grandmama . . .' He stepped forward, bending a little to twinkle at her, to humour her.

Seeking more support she turned to the next person. 'Elizabeth, you've got a short-sleeved frock on. You must be cold!'

'Well . . . well . . . yes, I am. A little.'

'There!' said Mrs Winthorpe, triumphantly.

Brian took the matches from Father's smoking table and lit the fire before there could be any further argument.

Harry made for the thermometer. 'I'm going to confiscate this thing,' he announced.

'Oh, no,' cried Mrs Winthorpe. 'I like to look at it.'

'You look at it far too much.'

'I don't. I don't.'

Jack watched Harry carefully detach the thermometer and put it into his pocket, and it seemed to him as though Harry had been standing behind Father all these years just waiting to pop his feet quickly into Father's vacant slippers while they were still warm (leaving him, the eldest son, out in the cold).

'I shall buy another!' Mrs Winthorpe said under her breath as she settled herself in the corner of the sofa nearest the fire, which was beginning to crackle and burn merrily.

Harry sat down in the chair furthest away from the fire, then lifted himself out again to fetch his crochet from the writing table. He brought back with him one of the copies of the will which was lying on top of a blotter and handed it to Joanna.

'You might like to have a look at this,' he said.

Joanna pushed Nebuchadnezzar's feet into the more compact mass of his body and sat down on the cleared space on the fireside stool. She remembered Grandfather's feet resting on this stool. Such small, neat feet they were, for so large a man – a small black bow jaunting on the dulled patent leather of each shoe, and tidily clocked ankles leading up into the enormous bulk in purple smoking-jacket with gold-buttoned waistcoat and white pleated shirt front striped by the swinging black line of ribbon suspending his monocle, at his neck a larger edition of the black bow on each of his feet. Beside those neat little feet lay Nebuchadnezzar, grey like the rug which was always at hand to be flung over Grandfather's legs when they felt cold. Rug and cat were still there.

Brian helped himself to a cigarette from the box on Father's smoking table, glanced at the empty chair, paused, turned his back on it and started to bend his knees. Suddenly he straightened up and made for a chair on the opposite side of the room, walking quickly and humming a little tune.

Jack went and stood in front of the fire. His glance roved from the sleeping cat to the folded rug to the empty chair. Nearly all the other chairs in the room were occupied.

After all, somebody would have to sit in Father's chair, sometime.

Who, if not he, was truly entitled . . .?

He approached it gallantly but, just as he was about to take it, shied. Not yet! He grabbed a cigarette from Father's box and went to squeeze himself in between Laurine and Elizabeth on the sofa.

'Can you understand it all? The will, I mean?' Mrs Winthorpe asked Joanna.

'Yes, I think so,' she said slowly. 'I think so. . . .'

Uncle Jack's share of Grandfather's money in trust so that he could not use it as he wished, could only receive the income from it. 'An actress – so unsuitable' came the echo of a whisper after Uncle Jack had announced his marriage. So this was how Grandfather had expressed his disapproval (even though after the marriage he had been quite pleasant to Laurine): with a relentlessness that was somehow shocking even though it *was* his money. . . .

And her own share – in trust. So Grandfather had known, after all, about Tony? She wondered what he would have said if she could have told him about Tony and the hot-water tap. Would he have laughed, too?

She turned to her grandmother. 'Do you understand it?' she asked, wondering if her grandmother would understand the implications of that 'in trust', but despairing even as she hoped because she remembered the many times she had been told what a lucky girl she was to have such a wonderful husband.

'I haven't seen it.'

'Haven't seen it? Haven't seen the will? But . . .'

'Oh, I don't mind,' Mrs Winthorpe said wearily. Harry going off like that, with the thermometer in his pocket, had filled her with disquiet. She had so looked forward – wickedly, perhaps, and perhaps she would be punished for her wicked-ness – to a little peace after Alfred was . . . if ever she was left alone. She had thought of leading her own life at last, free from grumbles, free to go out without having to ask every time for permission to use the car and being sneered at: 'What for this time? Going to gossip with your friends? Or going to get your hair done again? Thought you'd had a *permanent* wave!' Alfred never could understand, and she had tried over and over again to explain, that it *was* permanent but still had to be set into its wave each time it was washed. Then, Alfred would say, it is not a permanent wave. There's nothing per-manent about it! Oh, yes, Alfred! It is! There is! She got so tired of trying to explain. Year after year. And now here was Harry. Popping the thermometer into his pocket. Her mind clutched in dismay at her peach bath. Perhaps he wouldn't let her have one after all, and she wanted a peach bath so badly. Peach, not pink. Pink was rather vulgar.

Joanna saw the weariness on her grandmother's face, and realised that she was too tired, after all these years, to protest any more. The complaints, displeasures, threats not always veiled, which had closed in on her day by day, month by month, year by year, throughout that long, long marriage, had gradually stifled even the faint tentative fluttering she might once have made towards freedom, while she had still been young enough and strong enough to escape. Now, she was beaten.

This could have happened to me! Joanna thought.

She looked at Tony, seeing him quite clearly, perhaps for the first time: a man who had caught a wild bird, blinding it so that it would sing for him better in the dark. Slowly, with deliberate cunning, he had edged his darkness down upon her, biding his time until the day when she would sing any tune he called – 'Your money, sweet . . .' she could hear him saying it! '. . . let me handle it for you. You know how careless you are, sweet!' – only, he had bargained without the singing bird regaining its sight!

How lovely to see again! To sing one's own song, to be free!

'I think I'll go to bed,' said Mrs Winthorpe. She sighed, and stood up.

They all rose except Harry, who was asleep in his chair, his mouth slightly open and his crochet trailing over his slack knees.

Brian kicked him gently.

'What!' said Harry, giving a great start so that the crochet fell off his knees and the reel of cotton went bowling off along the carpet, unwinding itself as it went, to disappear under the sofa. 'Oh, blast! Now look what you've done.'

'I haven't done anything. It was you. You were asleep.'

'Should think so too, with the heat of this room.' Harry went down on his knees to rescue his crochet.

'Hadn't you better read this in bed, Granny?' Joanna offered Mrs Winthorpe the copy of the will which she had finished reading.

'Oh . . . thank you. . . .'

'Goodnight, Mother,' Jack said very cordially, speeding her on her way because then he could get down to the main business of the evening. He had thought it better to wait until Mother had gone to bed before going into the details of the will with Harry and Brian.

'Goodnight.'

'Goodnight.'

'Goodnight.'

Harry, Brian and Joanna – as Mrs Winthorpe kissed them she rested her hands briefly on each pair of shoulders – the strong shoulders of her family! – bent to kiss Laurine's cheek, briefly; kissed Elizabeth, less briefly; was encircled for a moment by Tony's arms, then went on her way. She turned back from the pool of shadows in the doorway to cry once more 'Goodnight' to all, and for an instant her face seemed to float disembodied, tender and luminous, above the black velvet of her gown.

'Now,' Jack began, as soon as they had all resettled themselves. 'There are just one or two questions I should like to ask regarding my position . . .'

'There is another matter which I really do think comes first in importance,' Harry interrupted.

'Oh?' asked Jack. 'And what's that?' What *could* be more important?

'The ashes.'

'What about them?'

'We don't quite like the idea of scattering them,' said Brian.

'You remember how Brian had to scatter poor Uncle James,' Elizabeth reminded them. 'From Beachy Head. And Uncle James blew back in his face.'

'There's always a fearful wind on Beachy Head,' said Jack.

'Poor Brian. It was dreadful for him. He was so fond of Uncle James.'

'Of course it's not so windy here . . .' ruminated Jack.

'No, but still . . . It seems a little undignified, somehow, this . . .' Brian broke off to imitate, very gracefully, a scooping and scattering motion.

Joanna stood up and stretched. The stool was not very comfortable, and Grandfather's chair was empty. She sat down in it. Although a feeling of intense uneasiness came over her she sat quite still, stretching her arms along the solid plushed arms of the chair and pressing her back against the cushions. She sensed the ripples of uneasiness ringing outwards round the family. At last the rippling repercussions subsided, and she relaxed, her arms growing limp and sliding down gently into her lap. Hooking her heel over the cross-bar

of the stool she drew it close, put her feet on it (as Grandfather used to) and coolly met Nebuchadnezzar's green look which seemed perhaps to accuse, certainly to query.

'I see what you mean about scattering,' said Jack at last.

'The point is,' Harry said, 'the urn from the crematorium has to be buried in the family plot in the churchyard, and just a few of the ashes are to be taken out and scattered by the old shrine. And if we are not going to scatter them . . .'

'Wouldn't it be all right to scatter them if there are only going to be a few?' Jack put in.

'There won't be that few!' said Brian.

'. . . if we are not going to scatter them,' Harry repeated, 'we must find something to put them in.'

'A little jar?' Jack suggested helpfully.

There was silence while they all thought about a jar.

Then Jack said: 'What about his cigarette box? Wouldn't that be rather nice? I mean, he made it himself. . . .'

'Yes,' said Harry. 'That's a further possibility.'

'Hmm,' said Brian.

Joanna felt great bubbles of laughter gathering inside her, joining one another, welling up and up. . . .

'Yes, that seems quite a good idea,' Harry said again.

The laughter threatened to overflow and Joanna could sit still no longer. She reached out for a cigarette – from his box. And the laughter burst from her in low chuckles.

They stared at her, Jack, Harry, Brian, Laurine, Elizabeth and Tony. Slowly, a sheepish smile spread across each face, broadened, became a grin, broke into a chuckle, a laugh; and died into silence.

'It's so – so small,' Joanna said at last. 'Besides, you can't! Not his own cigarette box!'

No. Perhaps she was right. Perhaps not his cigarette box. Father's wishes. He could scarcely have intended when he made that box that it should ever be used for such a purpose.

'I'll tell you what,' Jack exclaimed. 'Why not get hold of old what's-his-name, old Jordan, to make a box in the morning? He used to be a bloody good carpenter in his spare time.'

'Yes!' Brian was enthusiastic. 'Now that *is* a good idea.'

Jack enjoyed Brian's approval. Then Harry added his own approval. Jack basked, until he was interrupted by Elizabeth saying she thought she would go on up to bed.

Harry wished to goodness the women would all go up to bed at the same time instead of in relays. All this getting up and down. He rose, stretched himself slightly, blinked, wished Elizabeth goodnight and sank thankfully back into his chair again.

There was a faint crack in his right pocket.

'Hell!' he said, getting up again quickly.

The others looked at him in surprise. 'What is it?'

'The blasted thermometer!' He removed the pieces of broken glass from his pocket and showed them round in silence. He dared anyone to laugh! Then he removed his dinner jacket and held it upside down while he waved it vigorously to and fro.

Joanna began to shake with silent laughter. It was different from the laughter that had shaken her when she reached for a cigarette from Grandfather's box. Happiness was suddenly within her reach. With Andrew she would be able to laugh.

'What *are* you doing?' Brian asked.

Harry compressed his lips and didn't answer. Mercury, he was saying to himself. Those little balls of mercury. Skipping around in his pocket and turning his gold signet ring to silver if he put his hand in his pocket.

He shook his jacket harder than ever, and was rewarded by a minute silver shower.

'Now they'll run all over the place!' Brian scolded. 'It's the very devil, that stuff!'

Laurine began a little trill of laughter, and Harry nipped it with a frown.

He turned back to Brian: 'No, they won't. They'll disappear into the pile of the carpet.' He rubbed his foot over the carpet to help them.

'Don't you believe it! They'll go running all over the floor and Upjohn will have a hell of a time chasing them with a dustpan.'

'I don't care what sort of a time Upjohn has! They're not staying in my pocket!'

Brian caught Joanna's eye and his lips twitched.

'They'll suddenly pop out from under the blue sofa and roll merrily across to Father's chair. Like that old spider used to.'

'Oh, yes!' said Joanna. 'I remember that spider. What was it we used to call him? Wasn't it a Mister Somebody?'

'Oh, it was a Mister *Somebody*. Mister . . . Mister . . . ?'

Harry shrugged himself back into his dinner jacket, frowned at everybody – how dare they laugh! – rubbed his foot firmly over the carpet to make sure there was no chance of any mercury popping up from anywhere to roll anywhere, and sat down again, this time more carefully.

'Let's turn to something a little more important than trying to remember the name of a spider, shall we?' he said.

'Well, there's one question I particularly wanted to ask,' Jack said quickly. 'Is my . . .?'

'Christman!' Brian interrupted him loudly.

'What do you mean, Christman?' demanded Jack, trying not to speak irritably.

'Christman was that spider's name. I've just remembered.'

'*Mister* Christman!' Joanna corrected him.

'Oh, well, of course,' said Harry huffily, 'if you're going to insist on playing the giddy goats . . .' Bits of broken glass and mercury all over his pocket, and now this! It really was abominable. 'May I remind you that we have not yet finished discussing the ashes?'

Brian said soothingly: 'We're not playing giddy goats. But I thought we had decided Jordan would make a little box tomorrow morning?'

'I'll go and see about it first thing,' Jack said with alacrity. He remembered Harry, and added: 'Shall I?' If only they could get this settled and get on to the important part of the discussion.

Harry agreed. It was settled. Jack opened his mouth . . .

'Just a minute!' Brian raised his right hand.

Jack shut his mouth. His foot began to jerk up and down in the air, and Laurine kicked him on the ankle gently.

'Wood perishes,' said Brian. 'Worms. And dry rot.'

'Well?' Harry enquired tersely.

'It just seems rather a pity that the box will rot away and the ashes will all be mixed up with the earth.'

'Well, considering the original suggestion was to scatter them . . .'

'I know. But as we have now decided to bury them it might be a good plan, I feel, to put them in a jar, or a bottle, which will last for ever, and put *that* inside the box. It seems rather a pity not to do a job thoroughly.'

The exceptional mildness of his tone did not deceive Jack. Brian's tone invariably became milder with the stiffening of his attitude. It considerably shortened a family argument to throw in one's hand early on the winning side.

Jack said: 'I do so agree with you. Preserve them for posterity.'

'In my opinion . . .' began Harry, was met by the implacable blue gaze which Brian levelled at him, paused, then finished less positively: 'Well – a glass jar inside the box might perhaps be best. A small jar. With a stopper, of course.'

'Yes,' said Brian. 'That's just what I thought. Father's name and date of birth can be written in indelible ink on a slip of paper and put inside it. That would be legible centuries from now. . . .'

. . . A man is digging beside the ruins of an old shrine. Suddenly he pauses; the edge of his spade has struck something hard. He bends down and grubs with his fingers in the earth until they encounter a small, smooth object. He lifts it and brushes from it the rich crumbs of caked soil. The dull, thick glass appears and through it, blurred and obscured as by a wall of water, can be seen a grey powdery substance. The man holds up the object and the sunlight falls upon it for the first time in many hundreds of years; frowning and squinting he examines it keenly. With difficulty he reads the ancient writing on the small slip of yellowed paper in the jar: 'These are the last mortal remains of Alfred Winthorpe. . . .' His heart beats rapidly with excitement at such a find. Tomorrow he will take it to the Museum. . . .

. . . 'But we still have to find a jar,' said Jack. 'Have you anything suitable among your photographic stuff, Harry?'

'We don't need to use a second-hand jar. Brian and I will go into town tomorrow and buy one while you go and speak to Jordan about making the box. He'll have it ready by midday if you go immediately after breakfast.'

Blast! thought Jack. He would have to walk all the way to Jordan's cottage and back if Harry and Brian were going off in Harry's car. No. He could ask Tony to drive him down. Tony was always ready to do anyone a good turn.

'Is that settled, then?' he asked. 'You get the jar. I get the box. Right?'

'Yes,' said Brian.

'Yes,' said Harry.

Tony looked at the clock. Three-quarters of an hour to discuss one small glass jar and one wooden box!

Jack waited until he was sure there were not going to be any further interruptions about bloody Christman or the ashes. Then he said: 'It looks to me – I don't know whether I'm right or not – but it looks to me as if I shall have nothing

to leave my widow except what I can make myself out of my paintings.'

Laurine looked at him, startled. What was this?

'Yes,' said Harry. 'I'm afraid that is so.' He didn't altogether agree with Father's harshness, but after all it was the Old Man's money and he could do what he liked with it.

'The way I understand it, the capital from which I have the income for life is to be divided after my death among you, Brian and Joanna, and my widow will not see a penny of it? Right?'

Little nudges of indignation had been playing on his mind like sundry notes on a piano ever since he had first read the will, before tea. Now, as he put his construction of the will into actual words, he felt them all strike together in a veritable chord of anger.

Why should Laurine be treated like this? What was wrong with being an actress – and a good actress at that? He was damn proud of her. . . .

'I'm afraid that is so,' said Harry again. 'As you have no children. If you had, it would of course have gone to it. Or them.'

. . . damn proud to have a child of hers, too! He'd show them all how proud he was of her!

To have a child . . . well, after all, why not? He was not all that old. And it was up to him, really, as eldest son, to perpetuate the family. He should have thought of that before. He was not old at all! He put his arm round Laurine.

'Oh, darling, you big silly!' Laurine rubbed her cheek against his dinner jacket. 'Don't talk about me being a widow.

You're not going to die for ages and ages! And anyway,' she added, 'you could always take out some insurance.'

'I think it's rather unkind, to say the least of it.' Jack looked at Harry quite firmly over Laurine's head. 'But if I had to go back and have another chance, I'd still marry Laurine and be damned to the consequences.'

'Don't worry, darling, you can take out some insurance,' Laurine said again, a little more loudly.

Jack did not answer. He was still looking firmly at Harry. Then he looked at Brian.

Yes, thought Brian, the old boy certainly has quite a lot of dignity – and at a time when it must be bloody difficult for anyone to be dignified, too.

'Joanna's money is left in the same way, you know,' Harry explained.

'Well, that's different. Joanna's a woman. She hasn't got to think of providing for a widow. 'He paused. 'But why . . .?'

'It's very usual,' Harry said quickly, 'for a girl to have money in trust for her children if she has any and if not for it to come back into the family. After all, if it was left outright as Brian's and mine has been any unscrupulous fellow could get his hands on it and family fortunes could go in the wrong direction altogether.'

'But Uncle Harry,' said Joanna, watching Tony's face maintaining a pleasant expression as she slowly said her piece, 'I was married to Tony when Grandfather made that will, so why should he have still tied the money up in case, as you suggest, of an unscrupulous fellow?'

Not a hint of Tony's feelings spoiled his smile. How he had perfected his pose, thought Joanna. Smooth, gentle, charming, kindly – come a little closer, my dear! – and under the frilly nightcap the wolf – all the better to gobble you up with, my dear! She giggled.

'Oh, well – well – it's just the usual way for a girl. You must take my word for it, Joanna. What are you laughing at?'

'Nothing, Uncle Harry. Nothing at all. Really.'

There was a small silence, into which shot: '*Could you not take out some insurance?*'

This time Jack could not fail to hear.

'Yes, I suppose I could do that,' he said. 'But at my age one has to pay such high premiums. But don't worry, darling. I'll take care of you.'

'I don't know about anyone else,' Brian announced, 'but I'm dry! I could do with a glass of beer. I think I'll go along to the pantry and get some.' He waited, hoping someone else would make the move. He was very comfortable where he was.

Harry swallowed the bait. 'I'll go,' he said, pushing aside his crochet and getting to his feet. He was not going to have someone else messing about in *his* pantry.

'Can I help you, Harry?' said Tony.

'Yes, as a matter of fact, you can.' Good. Harry had been wanting an opportunity all evening for a few words alone with Tony.

XI

Harry took four bottles of beer out of the refrigerator and put them on a tray while Tony fetched the glasses.

'Shall I carry the tray?' asked Tony.

'In just a moment. But first I was going to tell you something which you may be glad to know.'

He paused to give effect to his words.

Tony felt his impatience rise and increase with the length of the pause. Was this, at last, some reward for the visit he had made to Harry six weeks ago?

At last Harry said: 'Father, as you know, was a very wealthy man . . .'

Yes, Tony knew that all right.

'. . . and left Joanna's money in trust.' He paused again.

Exasperated by Harry's deliberation, Tony ceased to concentrate on words which must be only a preamble to the objective he felt must surely be reached sometime – after all his trouble! – and he stood the monotone of '. . . avoid death duty . . . delegated to a committee . . . power to alter . . . terms and conditions . . .' as he might have sat out a train journey carrying him towards an anxiously awaited destination far more vivid in his consciousness than the meaningless and dull countryside through which he had to pass to get there.

'Brian and I . . . request the committee . . . so that Joanna will receive her income only so long as she remains married to you.'

It jolted him to a full stop – at the wrong destination.

Joanna to receive her income only so long as she remained married to him?

Christ, what were these fools up to now?

Supposing he found he couldn't stick Joanna any longer (there were other women just as attractive with just as much money and he could always do anything he liked with women). Supposing, just supposing, Joanna were ever in a position to divorce him – not that she'd ever catch *him* out, he'd take good care of that! – but just *supposing* she were able to, and her income was to end with the ending of their marriage? He'd have to pay her alimony – and she might not marry again.

Harry watched Tony's expression for the signs of gratitude he felt sure would be forthcoming. But to his surprise they didn't materialise.

When at last he was able to trust himself to speak, Tony said: 'Harry . . . er . . . you did say you and Brian were going to arrange things so that Joanna receives her income only so long as she remains married to me, didn't you?'

'Yes,' said Harry. 'That's right. That's what you want, isn't it? You want – we all want – to do everything possible to preserve your marriage.'

'Oh, of course,' said Tony. He carefully rearranged the glasses on the tray. Then he said: 'But Harry, I'm not sure that it's quite fair to tie someone down like that.'

He willed Harry to see him as a noble and generous man – his life for Joanna's (God damn her eyes!).

Not fair? Why the dickens not? If Father had known about this other man he'd have cut her out, right out. But Harry didn't want to do that. He was fond of Joanna, he wanted to give her another chance to be happy – he was sure she would be happy when she came to her senses. He was just going to make sure that she did come to her senses.

'Well, all I can say is,' Harry insisted, 'that if Father had known about her – her goings-on . . .' he nodded significantly '. . . he'd have punished her much more severely. He'd have cut her right out of the will altogether.'

Tony silently thanked God that the old bastard had not known. He hadn't thought of that aspect when he had gone to Harry to enlist his help and through him the eventual help of the entire Winthorpe family to bind Joanna to him. What a misjudgement! He must be more careful in future.

'I think that would have been a little harsh,' Harry went on. 'But all the same, she must be made to see sense. She's always been a bit wild, so was her mother – that disastrous marriage – but she's not really bad, you know.'

'Oh, of course not!' Tony was careful to keep his voice even and considerate. 'God knows I love her,' he said, and thought: the bitch! 'God knows I want her to spend the rest of her life with me. I'm willing to give her another chance. But isn't this thing you propose a little – drastic?'

'No. No, I don't think so,' said Harry, busying about with the beer bottles on the tray. He looked at Tony once again to make quite sure that Tony was not grateful – or at least not as grateful as he had expected.

Something was bothering him a bit. What was it that Brian had said? Was he, Harry, sure that Tony was a good husband, that he could be trusted? He hesitated for a moment, tapping

the bottle opener on the rim of a glass. Then he put it down on the metal tray with a decisive click to close any further argument among his thoughts. Of course Tony was to be trusted.

He picked up the tray and bustled off towards the hall, saying rather sadly to himself that Tony might have been a bit more pleased at what they were proposing to do to keep his marriage together. After all, he loved Joanna, he said. But there! People didn't always behave as they should, and he, at least, was sure he was doing the right thing.

Bother these shoes, he thought, how they squeak! And there was Tony, close behind him – he could feel Tony's eyes on his back and the feeling made him most uncomfortable. He wriggled his shoulders and wondered what one did for squeaky shoes. Vaseline? Olive oil?

XII

Joanna slid out of bed very quietly. Tony was breathing heavily in the next bed and seemed already safely asleep. She didn't want to wake him to the rage which she could tell, in spite of his careful concealment, had been boiling up inside him ever since he came back from getting the beer with Uncle Harry. What had happened, she wondered, to cause it?

She opened the bedroom door without a sound and trod lightly out onto the landing. The thick pile of the carpet brushed softly against her bare feet. How clean and fresh it felt outside that room, where she had been shut in with Tony and his anger.

A thin white line of light showed beneath one of the far doors, slicing into the darkness of the corridor and spreading over the oak floorboards in a narrow, gleaming pool of light. It was the door of Jack and Laurine's room. As she neared it on her way towards the stairs she heard their voices murmuring; ceasing; murmuring. She was filled with sudden pity for those voices sounding out of the darkness, lost, tender, unprotected.

She went down the inky pit of the stairs, stepping carefully and avoiding with precise knowledge the part of each step which would creak if trodden on – just as she used to when as a child she had crept out of bed and downstairs to listen at the dining room door to the laughter and chatter of a dinner party in progress.

At the foot of the stairs she paused, listening. Here again were all the sounds of the old house at night. Those sounds known and absorbed since childhood: the grandfather clock in the well of the stairs beating beside her like the giant heart of a person falling into sleep: steadily but losing, now and again, one beat, then with a great starting lurch, turning over once more to beat slowly, steadily, inevitably. The oak panelling giving sudden cracks as it contracted in the cooling darkness after the heat of the day. The drawing room clock chiming lightly, frivolously. The groan of a reluctant window being forced open and Uncle Harry's wireless still sounding from far off. A distant cough – not Grandfather's – a grunt, a sniff, a snore from those sleepers above, harmless behind closed doors, a sigh even – no, a little breeze which started up suddenly to blow through someone's open window, breathe beneath their door, and as suddenly to die.

She went through the hall, feeling her way along the walls and avoiding the furniture. The warmth of the dead fire was still imprisoned in the room. She reached the library and stepped inside the door to turn on the light. The furniture was still pushed back, leaving the empty, rectangular space in the middle of the room. For an instant she saw the coffin there, filling the empty space.

Tomorrow, she remembered, he would be coming back again. For the last time. Tomorrow would be the end of him.

She pushed open the French window and stepped out on to the terrace.

Light from two windows only flooded out across the garden, laying barred pathways across the lawn, silvering the leaden urns from which the geraniums leapt like small flames in the night. No light came from Harry's window, and the sound of his music had ceased now; her grandmother's room too was unlit. And as she looked along the house one of the two remaining lighted windows subsided into darkness and the centre room alone, Uncle Jack's room, still streamed light from its open window – inside, those voices would still be murmuring, perhaps. Love talk, perhaps. Andrew! she thought, and pressed her arms tight against the fullness of her breasts.

For a long time she stood looking up at the old house which had been her home for twenty years, which now contained all her family – and Tony.

Tomorrow, she would have to tell them about Tony, tell them that she could no longer live with him. She would have to face them all, and make them understand about Andrew. And whatever they said, she knew now that it would make no difference. It would not alter her decision. It was her life – her decision. She had lived her life too long in the shadow. Now. she had recovered her strength.

'Remember, if ever you want me, I shall be there.' It was almost as if Andrew had spoken again – here, now, on the terrace – those last words he said to her. He was beside her now, and the way was clear for both of them. Tomorrow, she would telephone him. Soon, very soon, she would be with him.

THE FOURTH DAY

I

'Joanna!'

At the sound of Tony's voice she was instantly alert, but she buried her face in the pillow, murmuring with pretended drowsiness which had been real until he spoke. For a moment she felt the flick of the old, familiar fear: then she reminded herself that soon she would be talking to Andrew again. The fear vanished.

She lifted her head and looked at Tony. 'What is it?' she asked. She realised from the half-smoked cigarette between his fingers that he must have been awake some minutes, although she herself had not even heard Upjohn come in with the tea.

He stared at her for a few seconds in silence. Then he said: 'Never mind. It's nothing.' He stubbed out his cigarette. Rouse her curiosity: then let her sweat a bit. Pick the moment when it's good and ripe. Then let her have it.

The last day, thought Joanna as she threw back the bed-clothes. But for me – the first. The first day without fear. . . .

Tony said: 'I heard something last night which you might find very interesting.'

. . . For Grandfather, the last day. Soon, in a few hours, it will all be over: the last trace gone, buried. Slowly the memory losing its strength as he lost his from day to day, dying; depending for brief revival on our minds and memories and when we too are dead becoming no more than a name on a bit of paper in a bottle. . . .

'What?' she said.

'Very interesting. So interesting, in fact, that I couldn't sleep all night wondering whether to tell you.'

She paused on the edge of the bed, remembering his heavy-breathing sleep of last night when she had crept out of the room away from him. 'What is it, then?'

Tony was watching her and she reached quickly for her negligée.

'Well . . . it's very interesting . . . for you.'

'Yes. So you said before. Why don't you tell me what it is?'

'What'll you do for me if I tell you?'

Tony's glance licked round the folds of her negligée; she drew it more tightly round her and stood up.

'Don't you want to know, sweet? Don't you think you ought to know? After all, it's for your own good.'

'If you think I ought to know, then tell me.' From habit she held her arms folded in front of her, ready to tense and press them against her body to control its usual reaction of panic to his baiting.

'But you see, sweet, it's not really fair that I should do

something for you if you're not prepared to do something for me, is it? Surely even you can see that?'

There was no panic, no sign of panic. She let her arms fall to her sides and wondered how she could ever have been taken in by him.

'If, for instance, you were to come into my bed . . . I could talk to you so much better in my bed.'

She controlled her disgust with an effort: disgust with him, disgust with herself for ever having been taken in by him. But why look at the past? The future was all that mattered now.

'If you can only tell it me in bed, then I'd rather not hear it,' she said. She picked up her clothes. 'I'm going to have a bath.'

As she went out of the room she said: 'And as I'm going to have a bath in Jack's bathroom, you'd better be sure to turn the hot-water tap off.'

II

As Joanna went along the corridor to her grandmother's room she saw Brian and Elizabeth going in, and at the same time Jack and Laurine coming out.

'Morning!' Jack touched two fingers to his forehead in a gay salute as he passed her, and Laurine smiled so brightly and sweetly that Joanna wondered. Particularly she wondered when she remembered last night and 'could you not take out some insurance' and, later, those lost voices sounding out into the darkness.

Mrs Winthorpe was sitting up in bed with the will spread out on the uncrumpled sheet in front of her. Brian and Elizabeth bent solicitously over her.

'Outcasts!' she cried. 'We're outcasts, Jack and I!'

'Oh, come now, Mother. It's not as bad as that,' Brian comforted her.

'What do you mean, Granny?' Joanna asked.

'Well, Sylvia – I mean Joanna – I'm not an executor . . . surely the widow is usually an executor? All the ones I know are – were. And even worse, Jack's not an executor. The eldest son! Oh, I think it's dreadful!'

'But Mother,' Brian said, 'surely you knew this before – that Harry and I were the only executors?'

'No, I . . . oh, I had heard you talking, I suppose . . . but Father never consulted me about anything, you know what he was like . . . and now seeing it in black and white. . . . Oh, I don't mind for myself. But Jack. Poor darling. It's such a dreadful humiliation.'

Uncle Jack didn't look humiliated, thought Joanna. In fact, he looked surprisingly cheerful this morning.

'Of course,' continued Mrs Winthorpe, 'Alfred – Father – always threatened that when his time came Jack would have a nasty jar. All because of Laurine, poor little creature. Of course, one wouldn't have chosen . . . but she's a nice little thing . . . I never thought Al . . . Father could really mean it. After all it couldn't possibly have hurt to have had three executors. Or even four. It's so cruel.' Tears stood in her eyes.

'Well, I'm afraid there's nothing we can do about it,' said Brian helplessly. Not that he wanted to be an executor anyway

– he was a busy man – and he was sure Mother was imagining Jack's being humiliated. Why, the old boy had taken things extremely well, Brian thought. And good luck to him!

'And worst of all he's got nothing to leave his widow.'

'He's got his paintings, and what he makes from them,' Brian reminded her.

'Yes, but . . .' she lowered her voice, 'I never really thought Jack ought to be an artist. He paints very nicely, of course, but . . . I think he would have done far better to take up a profession. He's too old now, of course, so . . . I've decided to leave him all my money.'

'All your money?' said Brian.

'Yes. Oh, I know it's only about £20,000, and when the horrid government have been at it after I die there won't be much left. But it'll be better than nothing. I shall go down to Mr Trent this morning and do it right away. It's too important for a note in my glove drawer!'

There was silence.

Oh dear, thought Brian. Something certainly ought to be done for Jack if possible, especially as he's taken it so well. But this seems rather – drastic.

'I shouldn't be in too much of a hurry,' he cautioned.

'Oh, yes, yes!' cried Mrs Winthorpe. 'I've quite made up my mind. And I want to do it at once. One never knows when one is old. Although,' she added, and her voice became dispirited, 'I don't mind when I go. I think the world is horrible nowadays. These terrible wars and floods and earthquakes – it's all because people are so wicked nowadays with these dreadful atoms and things. In the old days . . . why, things

don't even taste the same now . . . potatoes and asparagus
. . . no, I don't mind when I go!'

'Poor Mother,' said Elizabeth.

There was a gentle knock on the door and Tony came in.

When he had said good morning to everybody he turned
to Joanna: 'I didn't know you'd come on without me, sweet,
I was waiting for you.'

'Were you?' she said.

Mrs Winthorpe hardly noticed Tony this morning. 'Jack
shall have that £20,000,' she repeated.

Twenty thousand pounds? thought Tony. What was this?

'I think it's terribly kind of you, Mother,' said Elizabeth,
and Brian echoed vaguely 'terribly . . .' as his mind took a
brisk turn around the problem.

Suddenly he brightened. Harry had suggested an alteration in the terms of Joanna's share, so there could just as
easily be an alteration in Jack's. Of course. Why on earth
hadn't he thought of it sooner?

There was a firm knock on the door and in came Harry.
As soon as she had kissed him Mrs Winthorpe said quickly,
almost defiantly: 'I'm going to leave Jack all my money!'

'I think it's a wonderful idea.' Elizabeth encouraged her,
just in case Harry should prove difficult.

But Brian frowned at her and broke into Harry's 'What
for?' with a gentle: 'That may not really be necessary, Mother.'

'Not necessary? But it is! It is! Something must be done,
and I'm going to do it at once. Jack is my eldest son.'

'I know he is, Mother, and he's our eldest brother, and we
all want to see him treated fairly. But there may be another

way of seeing that he is.' Brian looked meaningly at Harry, but Harry raised his eyebrows.

'I really don't see . . .' he began.

'I shall go to Mr Trent at once. At once,' Mrs Winthorpe insisted. She would not allow Harry (or Brian) to dissuade her. She was fighting now for her eldest son. Not for a thermometer. Not even for a peach bath. But for her eldest son.

'Now, Mother, Mother,' said Brian. 'Patience.' He ran the tip of his tongue over his lips. 'Harry,' he said, 'would it not be possible to – er – make a slight alteration in the terms of the trust settlement so as to allow Jack's money to go to his dependants after his death instead of to you, me and Joanna, then there would be no need for Mother to give up her poor little £20,000?'

'Yes,' said Harry, after consideration. 'That might be possible.'

But Mrs Winthorpe was still suspicious. 'Would that really be all right?' she enquired. 'Are you sure he'd have as much money to leave as you others?'

'Yes, of course,' said Brian. 'At least, as much as Harry and me. Joanna's comes back into the family, unless of course she has a child.'

Joanna avoided Tony's eyes.

'I must say,' began Mrs Winthorpe, 'I can't quite see why Father . . .'

Harry interrupted her. 'Mother, do let's stick to Jack, for the moment.'

'Yes, of course. I . . . Are you sure you can do this thing?'

'Oh, I think so. I think it can be managed,' said Brian.

'Yes, I don't see why not,' added Harry.

'I think we should start the ball rolling at once,' Brian went on.

Harry turned to Joanna. 'What about you, Joanna?' he asked. 'What do you feel about it?'

'Oh, I feel Uncle Jack should be able to leave his money to his widow if he wants to, of course I do. I really don't see why people shouldn't marry who they want, with all due respect to Grandfather. I certainly don't want any share of Uncle Jack's money.'

Tony made a sudden movement towards her, then checked himself. They were in public. But what a little fool she was! Jack wasn't a young man by any means, probably rogering himself to death every night anyway: that would mean another few hundred a year to her – to their – income if he'd got to be saddled with her for life anyway.

'And it really will be all right?' Mrs Winthorpe repeated.

Harry and Brian reassured her.

'It is a good idea, I think,' said Joanna. 'After all, you can't control people's lives by money – at least, you shouldn't.'

'The line must be drawn somewhere, though,' said Harry. Something was uncomfortable inside him for a moment, but he smoothed it down and patted it into place.

'But who has the right to draw it?' asked Joanna.

Her question went unanswered.

'Let's tell Jack at breakfast,' said Brian.

'No,' Harry objected. 'We'd better wait until it's finalised.'

'I don't think there's any doubt . . .' Brian began.

'Oh, if there is,' said Mrs Winthorpe, 'I shall go straight down . . .'

'There isn't any doubt!' said Brian.

Mrs Winthorpe sank back on her pillows. 'Jack will be so relieved. Poor darling.'

'Laurine will be pleased too, I should think,' said Brian. He looked at Joanna and 'Could you not take out some insurance?' leapt to her mind and she smiled. 'We might go and see Mr Trent for a few minutes this morning after we've bought the . . . after we've done that other job,' he finished, for his mother's benefit.

'We might do that,' Harry agreed.

Brian went to the door happily, his mind at rest. He was ready now for the sunny, upturned faces of fried eggs.

III

'Do you think we should get cracking?' said Jack. 'I mean, it'll take Jordan a little while to make the box, and there's not all that time left. Matthews has already gone off to the crematorium to fetch the ashes.'

Tony stifled a sigh. Couldn't one even finish one's after-breakfast smoke in peace? God, they'd hardly been out of the dining room five minutes!

'I suppose we should,' he replied pleasantly. 'Are you coming, Joanna?'

'No, I'm not. I've got a telephone call to make.'

He looked at her sharply. 'Who to?'

'Oh . . . just . . . a family matter.'

'A family matter, darling? Aren't I one of the family?' He laughed as though he had made a very funny joke, but Joanna merely repeated: 'Yes. A family matter' quite firmly, and didn't enlarge upon it.

He couldn't very well question her now, in front of people. But later on he'd get at her. He gave Laurine a dazzling smile: 'What about you? Are you coming with us?'

'No, I don't think so. Not this morning. . . .' She sent a shy look at Jack who explained: 'She's not feeling very strong this morning. She'll probably put her feet up for a bit after we've gone, won't you, darling? Hmm?'

'I can let you have some aspirin if you've got a headache,' said Elizabeth sympathetically.

'Oh, no, thank you . . . I haven't a headache. . . .' Again she looked at Jack and a secret smile passed between them, swift as a bird.

Harry came into the room, marched across to the piano, ruffled through the papers on top of it, turned round and marched out again without a word.

'I'll go and get the car,' said Tony.

Jack waited for him, holding Laurine's hand and playing with her fingers. 'I hope old Jordan will do a good job on this box,' he began conversationally. 'But there's not much time . . . .'

Harry came into the room again.

'I say,' he remarked, frowning. 'Has anyone seen *The Times*?'

'Yes,' Joanna replied. 'Uncle Brian said he wanted ten minutes' sweet silent session with it.'

'Oh, my God. I've been all over the house looking for the damned thing. Brian knows I always have it after breakfast. It really is insufferable.'

'He'll be out soon,' said Jack. 'He's been gone over five minutes already.'

Harry glanced at the clock and grunted. One couldn't depend on Brian in that respect. Besides, he couldn't wait.

'The *Express* is here,' Elizabeth offered.

'I prefer *The Times*,' said Harry shortly. Nevertheless, he took the *Express*, folded it neatly under his arm and made off.

Tony reappeared. 'Car's at the door, Jack.'

Jack kissed Laurine.

'Now you put your feet up for a while after we're gone,' he said. 'When I get back I shall have to dig a hole by the shrine so you'll have practically the whole morning to yourself.'

She smiled at him lovingly as he followed Tony out of the room.

As soon as the sound of the car had died away, Joanna stood up. 'I must go and make a telephone call,' she said.

Now that the moment had come at last she felt afraid: supposing he wasn't there? Supposing . . . Oh, stop supposing, she told herself, and made herself walk out of the room towards the library where she could telephone without being overheard. All the same, she envied Laurine and Elizabeth their happy tranquillity as they sat side by side on the sofa. Whatever troubles they might have, they at least were married to the man they loved. . . .

Elizabeth turned to Laurine as soon as they were alone.

'Are you sure you haven't a headache?' she said. What could be the matter with her?

'Quite sure.' Laurine got up and ran to the door. She peeped outside to make certain no one was within hearing, then carefully shut the door and came back to Elizabeth. 'Promise not to tell a soul if I tell you something?'

'Promise.'

'Well, Jack and I are going to have a baby!'

'A baby?' Elizabeth's eyes widened. 'When?'

'March.'

Elizabeth did a rapid and silent calculation. 'Late March?'

'Early!'

'But how do you . . . when did you . . .?'

'Last night,' said Laurine happily.

'But how can you . . . you can't possibly know yet!'

'Oh, yes. I am quite, quite sure. I just *know*. But please don't tell a soul, will you?'

'No, of course I won't breathe a word.'

'Jack would be very shocked if he knew I'd told you. But isn't it wonderful, wonderful that he really wants one at last?'

'Wonderful,' agreed Elizabeth, trying to sound convinced.

'And of course he'll want to tell everyone the news himself.'

'I shouldn't . . . would you tell everyone just yet?'

'Oh, no, we'll make quite sure first. But I *am* sure. It's just one of those things, you know. That's why I'm going to lie down. I don't think one can start being careful too soon, do you?'

'No, indeed.'

Laurine put her finger to her lips at the sound of firm, jaunty footsteps approaching.

Brian came in looking very pleased with himself.

'There,' he said, slapping *The Times* down happily on top of the piano. He shrugged to resettle his coat more comfortably. 'Now,' he announced, 'I'm ready for anything!'

'Darling,' Elizabeth began, 'Harry was just in here looking for *The Times*. He seemed rather put out. . . .'

'Oh, did he?' said Brian pleasantly. 'Well, he should have been a bit quicker on the uptake, shouldn't he?' He smiled. He felt absolutely in the pink. 'Did Harry want to do the crossword?' he asked slyly.

'No, I don't think. . . .' Elizabeth looked at Brian suspiciously, then she laughed. 'He just prefers *The Times* to the *Express* – and you know it!'

'Oh, well, it's a good thing he hasn't got *The Times*. He'd be more inclined to linger if he had, and we haven't got all that amount of time. Do you want to come into the town with us?'

'No, thank you, darling. As a matter of fact, I was just going upstairs with Laurine. She's not feeling awfully well.'

'Oh,' said Brian. Suspicion crept into his mind. 'Sick?' he enquired diffidently.

'No!' said Laurine quickly, giving Elizabeth a warning glance. 'Just – just – overtired, nerves, you know.'

'Ah,' said Brian. Suspicion went away.

'If she lies down for a little while she'll feel better,' said Elizabeth. 'And perhaps a couple of aspirins and some Cologne. . . .'

'Yes,' said Laurine gratefully. 'A couple of aspirins and some Cologne. . . .' And perhaps a little bismuth : she really did feel rather sick.

Harry came in looking very irritable.

'Brian,' he said. 'You might have told me you were going to make off with *The Times* like that. I was looking all over the house for it.' He slid the *Express* unobtrusively beneath the rest of the papers.

'Sorry,' said Brian breezily. 'I didn't know you wanted it.'

Then he ought to have known!

'I'm sorry if it cramped your style.'

'It didn't cramp my style at all. It's merely that I like to read *The Times* in the morning when I have a little leisure to do so.'

Brian was about to have a dig at the word leisure but he noticed Harry's crestfallen face and decided to drop the subject. 'Don't you think we ought to be on our way?' he said.

'Yes. Immediately.'

Brian winked at Elizabeth and followed Harry out of the room.

IV

Gently, Harry started the car into motion down the drive, changing gear slowly and carefully.

'Going straight to the chemist's?' asked Brian.

'I think so. They're almost certain to have what we want.'

'Oh, yes. They're bound to have all shapes and sizes of jars, I should think. You checked the size of the box with Jack, didn't you?'

'Of course.'

'After we've done that,' Brian continued, 'we'd better go straight on to Mr Trent. You are sure this plan of giving up our shares of Jack's money is feasible, aren't you? It'll save Mother a lot of trouble. And I really don't feel morally entitled to Jack's money.'

'No, nor do I. And I'm sure it can be done. After all, as we have the power. . . . We can arrange it so that Joanna is taken care of at the same time . . .' He paused and rubbed his moustache thoughtfully, then he went on: 'Do you know, when I told Tony last night of our plan he didn't seem grateful at all. Said something about no one having the right to tie Joanna up for the rest of her life.'

'Oh?' said Brian. 'I didn't know you were going to say anything to anyone yet. It's a little premature, isn't it? And, you know, Tony's an odd chap. I can't honestly say I've ever cared a great deal for him.' He had already decided to have a word with Mr Trent himself before anything was done about Joanna's money, although he hadn't yet said so to Harry.

'He's a grand chap!' said Harry. 'A good strong character. Just what Joanna needs. And kind as well.'

'Mm,' said Brian. 'Well, I can't say I've actually seen him being *un*kind, but . . .'

'And anyway, it's up to us to do something. . . . Father would have wished it, and we must carry out Father's wishes.'

Brian was silent for a few moments, then he said: 'On the other hand, you know, Father obviously *didn't* wish his money to go to Laurine, and here we are going off to arrange things so that it *will* go to her before he's even . . .'

Harry looked at him uneasily. He hadn't thought of that. Father's wishes. Blast. One tried to do one's best for everyone and look what happened.

'Well,' he said at last, unhappily scratching his head, 'it was your idea.'

'Yes. I know it was. But I've only just thought of this point. Let's see . . . it was Father's money, and he's surely entitled to leave it as he wished . . . we try to alter his wishes . . .'

Harry began to speak, but Brian held up a hand to silence him. He must not be interrupted. He was going somewhere, slowly. It would be all right in the end. . . .

'. . . but the money according to his wishes would come to us . . . when it comes to us it will be ours and we will be entitled to leave it as we wish . . .' he continued in a monotone, his eyes shut, thinking aloud '. . . we would presumably give it back to Laurine. . . .' He opened his eyes and concluded rapidly and cheerfully: 'So it doesn't really matter if we do it sooner rather than later. We're still only doing what's right.'

Harry felt happy again. Trust old Brian to hit on the right answer. He really was pretty efficient, however one might like to tease him at times.

'Yes,' he said. 'Of course we're only doing what's right.'

. . . such a good thing Jack is going to have his money to leave as he wishes, like the other sons, mused Mrs Winthorpe as she came downstairs. She was not quite clear what it was exactly that Harry and Brian had said they were going to do, but anyway the result would be (they had said so, hadn't they?) that Jack would be equal with them. That would make up to Jack a little for having been so slighted by Alfred.

'Poor darling,' she said aloud. 'Outcasts, that's what we are.'

She stopped speaking aloud as she made her way towards the drawing room. There would probably be someone in there and if they heard her coming alone talking to herself they would be bound to tease her – quite nicely, of course. All the same, it made one so conscious that one was getting old.

'Oh, where are they all?' she exclaimed as she opened the door and found the drawing room empty. 'Oh, gone to see about the little box, I suppose . . . and Harry and Brian were going to see about Jack's money. . . .'

She glanced at the clock. Ten past ten. This time tonight it would all be over. Everything would be gone.

She went to a vase of lilies which had been brought in from the library. No point in leaving it in the library. No one ever went in there now. She lifted the bunch a few inches, shaking it a little so that the sweet scent reached her afresh and a faint powdering of yellow pollen appeared on the shining white lower petals; she let the bunch settle back once more in the vase, slightly rearranged.

'Now where's my spectacle case . . .' she began and broke off quickly as the door opened.

'Oh, Elizabeth,' she said, relieved. She wouldn't mind if Elizabeth had heard her talking to herself. Elizabeth wouldn't laugh at her. 'Where is everybody?'

'Harry and Brian have gone into the town. Joanna went to make a telephone call, and I haven't seen her since, and Laurine is lying down.'

'Lying down?'

'Yes. Yes . . . er . . . she felt rather . . . well, nervy, I think . . . .'

'Nervy? How odd!'

'Jack and Tony have gone to see Jordan about the box for – for beside the shrine. Oh, here they are back again. I can hear their voices. . . .'

Jack and Tony came in.

'Jordan's going to make the box,' Jack announced. 'He had a lovely piece of oak he says he can use for it. It'll be ready in an hour or so. Rather a good show, don't you think?'

'Yes!' said Mrs Winthorpe, trying to emulate Jack's enthusiasm.

'I'll go and dig the hole by the shrine in a minute.' Jack rubbed his hands together and sank down into the sofa. He leaned his head back and closed his eyes. Mrs Winthorpe reminded herself that she really must put on another of Harry's crocheted antimacassars if people were going to lean their heads on the back of the sofa like that. She had thought they could manage without one, just for the short time during which the usual one was at the cleaners, but it was no good – she could see the pale-blue brocade of the sofa becoming grease-marked already. The drawing room was not really the place for the men to sit . . . it was a ladies room. Her room. But now they all seemed to prefer it, really, to the hall. They seemed to gravitate here. Perhaps that chair of Alfred's in the hall . . . empty . . . not liking to sit in it. . . .

Jack remembered suddenly that he hadn't walked all the way to and back from Jordan's cottage after all. There was no call for him to act tiredness. He opened his eyes and sat up.

'I heard Harry's car,' said Elizabeth.

'Did you?' Mrs Winthorpe lifted her head and listened. 'I didn't. And I'm not deaf, you know.'

'No, no, Mother, of course not.'

'I'll just have a look.' Jack got to his feet. 'Then we can go and choose a spot by the shrine.'

V

'I am most terribly grateful,' said Jack, turning first to Harry on one side of him, then to Brian on the other, as they trooped down the drive to prospect where beside the shrine the hole should be dug.

He tried to sound enthusiastic. On no account must their pleasure be spoiled, after all the trouble they had been to for his sake, by realising that he wasn't really worried anyway, that their sacrifice was unnecessary now because he was going to have a child. Besides, it was not absolutely certain yet that he was going to have a child – although he thought it highly improbable that he wouldn't. Look at Laurine: strong, healthy, bouncing little thing, just made to be a mother. And he was as fit as a fiddle.

'I never expected anything of this sort. It's damned good of you all.'

'Well, both Brian and I, and Joanna, feel we're not morally entitled to your money.'

Jack thought Harry looked rather disgruntled, but he put it down to embarrassment at being thanked.

'And Mr Trent says the alteration will be perfectly in order.'

Harry's frown deepened as he recalled Mr Trent's words: 'You can effect an alteration provided a signed request is obtained from all beneficiaries under the will, otherwise no alteration.' Ridiculous. Signed request, indeed.

That meant they had been powerless to do anything about Joanna. Powerless! She'd scarcely sign away her own income, even though it was for her own good, ultimately.

He felt more and more indignant as he thought about it. He had been so sure something could be done. Something *ought* to be done. For the sake of the family. For the sake of Joanna herself, if she'd only realise it, silly girl!

'I'm so glad it was possible,' said Brian. 'It did seem unfair.' And, he added to himself, I'm glad the other thing was impossible. I don't like the idea of tying Joanna up to Tony, scandal or no scandal. There's something about him . . . I don't know. . . .

'Here we are,' said Jack, as they reached the old shrine.

They circled round beside it, brushing away with their feet the dead leaves which had blown around it.

'Here, do you think?'

'Here?'

'Here?'

'Or here?'

Brian hovered, his glance raking quickly along the ground; he swooped, steadied, and with a circular movement of his foot scratched away the leaves until a bare patch of earth was exposed.

'Here,' he said, beckoning to Jack. 'This is the spot – here.'

Jack looked at Harry.

Harry nodded.

Jack came forward, tipped the shining silver-grey edge of

the spade into the naked soil and lifted his left foot on to the shoulder of the upright blade. He braced himself, leaned forward, bore down – and the steel plunged unwillingly into the stony resistance beneath.

VI

'Here they are,' said Mrs Winthorpe, watching them come back up the drive – Harry, his arms held away from his body, rolling a little in his walk; Jack striding along with the spade over his shoulder; Brian stepping briskly, his toes well turned out.

'They've been three-quarters of an hour,' she remarked to Joanna and Elizabeth, who joined her at the window. 'Poor Jack. It must have been such hard work. He looks so hot. And after the way Father treated . . .' She broke off.

'Did you find a place?' she enquired, as Jack came into the drawing room.

'Yes, it's ready. Now all we've got to do is to get the box from Jordan.'

'Would you like me to do that?' asked Tony.

'That's very kind of you . . .' said Jack.

'Yes, and you sit down for a while!' Mrs Winthorpe ordered Jack. 'You look tired out.'

'Not a bit of it. I'm as fit as a fiddle!' Jack started to brush a few specks of dirt from the turn-ups of his trousers.

Oh, not on the drawing room carpet! cried Mrs Winthorpe silently.

Jack turned to Joanna. 'Many thanks for your part in the agreement about this money of mine. It's a nice thought.'

'I'm glad it can be done.'

Tony listened with rage. Twenty-five thousand pounds given and accepted as casually as a cheap box of confectionery. Did money mean nothing to this damned family? It would, if they had come by it the hard way, as he had. Not that they'd ever know how hard he'd come by it . . . he'd been careful to show them a family tree as good as theirs any day, branching conveniently off to Australia half a century ago just in case they wanted to meet any of his relatives.

He stood up. 'I'll go then, and get the box.' He glanced at Joanna. She looked happier than he'd seen her look for a long time. What was she up to? He'd get hold of her later and find out. About that phone call, too.

'Where are Harry and Brian?' asked Mrs Winthorpe. She looked at Jack's head which was leaning back against the sofa again, and she thanked goodness that she had just placed there a nice, clean piece of Harry's crochet which could quite easily be washed.

'They went out to the garage for a few minutes.' Jack pictured them shovelling? shaking? tipping? Father into the jar.

VII

'Did they all go in?' Jack asked, as Harry and Brian and Tony came back into the drawing room. He roused himself to admire the box in Harry's hands.

'Enough,' said Harry. 'The rest stayed in the other casket, the one Matthews collected from the crematorium, for this afternoon's performance.'

Brian stared at Harry incredulously, then realised he was not intending to be funny.

And, after all, what else was it? Father's last performance. The final curtain.

Mrs Winthorpe came in wearing her large black hat, followed by Joanna, Elizabeth and Laurine, all hatless.

'What a beautiful little box!' Mrs Winthorpe went towards Harry to look more closely. Then she stopped. 'Is he . . .?'

'It's all ready to put by the shrine,' Brian said gently.

Mrs Winthorpe went no nearer. 'I suppose we ought to be going,' she said.

She went to the drawing room door which Harry held open for her, heard them all following behind her, Laurine, Elizabeth, Joanna. . . .

Jack came last, carrying the little box carefully, so as not to shake it.

Out in the courtyard Harry picked up the spade which was leaning against the wall of the house where Jack had left it. Harry shouldered the spade himself now, since Jack's hands were full.

In silence they walked down the drive. Their feet were loud on the gravel.

They came to the shrine.

'Well . . .' Jack hesitated. Should he put the box down, down into the earth? Now? They drew round him, standing in a circle, waiting. . . .

Joanna moved nearer. 'How beautifully Jordan has made the box,' she said gently, not seeing Jack but only the oak box he was holding. She put out her hand to touch the smooth,

sweetly-dovetailed joints and trace with her fingers the lovely grain of the wood which was like the eddying of many waters.

Jack held the box out to her and she took it from him. She felt the lightweight shock of it between her hands and sudden anguish ran through her. This, for all of us, is how life must end.

She gave the box back to Jack and stepped into her place in the circle.

'Shall I . . .?' Jack looked at Harry.

Harry nodded.

Jack knelt beside the hole, leaning forward. The little box in his outstretched hands hovered for a second over the dark opening in the earth. Then it was gone.

He stood up, empty-handed.

He took command then, and reaching for the spade from Harry he said: 'We will each throw in a spadeful of earth. Mother?'

'Yes, but – but you men do it. I don't think I will.' She stifled the urge to jump backwards away from the spade which Jack held out to her.

'Very well.' Jack lifted a spadeful of loose earth and let it slide gently into the hole. It fell with scarcely a sound.

Harry took the spade from Jack, filled it, threw the earth gently down the hole, and handed the spade to Brian.

Brian turned his spadeful into the hole, scraped the remaining crumbs of soil from where the little mound of excavated earth had lain and used them to level out the surface. He smoothed the earth down like a coverlet over someone asleep,

gently so as not to awaken them; earth to earth, ashes to ashes, dust to dust. Sleep well, poor tired old man.

Jack moved forward. Once more he knelt down and with his hand gently swept the dead leaves to cover the broken earth until no trace of disturbance was left.

'No one would ever know . . .' said Mrs Winthorpe.

VIII

As Mrs Winthorpe left the dining room after lunch she said to Joanna: 'I'd like your opinion on a black hat for this afternoon. I don't want to wear the one I had on this morning . . . . I wore it all day yesterday. There's one which I put away sometime ago for jumble or Cousin Laura, but I've been looking at it again and it really seems quite fashionable now. Only I'd like you to see it on first.'

'Can I come too, Grandmama?' Tony asked.

Mrs Winthorpe looked at him with slight surprise.

'Yes, of course,' she said. 'If you'd really be interested!'

'I would be. I like to see girls trying on things!'

'Oh! Girls!' Mrs Winthorpe gave a self-conscious laugh. 'Come along then.'

Joanna and Tony followed her upstairs.

As they walked along the corridor Joanna stopped to look, as she had so often looked before, at the two coloured caricature sketches which hung on the wall.

Mrs Winthorpe saw her smile.

'Oh, those pictures of Grandfather and me. Aren't they dreadful? But he would have them hung there.'

Joanna stared at the caricature of her grandmother – upright, immaculate, the pain of an artificial smile twisting her lips, her whole expression somehow bewildered, taken aback; and at the caricature of Grandfather, merry and carefree as Joanna had never once seen him in reality, his moustache seeming to curl gaily instead of to bristle, his hat tilted, and his stick raised in jaunty greeting.

Mrs Winthorpe said: 'They're dreadful things. I hate them.'

'But they were taken on your honeymoon!'

'Yes, I know. In Paris.' On the morning after he had taken me to one of those places, red lights and red velvet, everything red; and peepholes. Horrible. Horrible.

'Grandfather looks as if he's enjoying himself anyway.'

'Yes, I suppose he does.' He never ought to have taken me to a place like that. It was very wrong. Only nineteen and I didn't know a thing. What a shock.

'What had you been up to?'

'Nothing! We were on our honeymoon.' She was never going to tell anyone about that hot dark red place. Never.

Tony sniggered. Nothing! On her honeymoon! He tried to catch Joanna's eye, moved nearer to her so that his arm touched hers.

She moved away at once. 'Shall we go and look at your hat, Granny? We haven't got a lot of time.'

Mrs Winthorpe flustered along the corridor after Joanna. She would take those horrible pictures down now!

Tony fondled his chin as he followed them. Those caricatures were rum objects. The old man looked as if he might

have been quite a sport once. What had turned him so sour? Her? She looked haughty as hell. Couldn't have been much fun to take to Paris! His mind peeped up the skirts of girls dancing the cancan.

Mrs Winthorpe lifted the lid off the cardboard hatbox on her bed, removed a fluttering, whispering sheet of tissue paper and drew out a small black hat with a cockade of ribbon at one side.

Joanna eyed it dubiously. 'Isn't it a little small?'

'Miss Meacham says they're wearing them small this year. She's remodelling my red straw, the one I bought at Southport – of course, I shan't be able to wear that just at present – and this black one didn't look at all bad when I tried it on before lunch. I put it on straight, tilted a little over the forehead, not to one side as I used to wear it.' She turned to Tony, explaining: 'Hats were fashionable worn to one side when I bought it.'

Tony nodded, pretending deep interest.

Mrs Winthorpe took up her stance in front of the mirror and settled the hat on her head.

'There!' She swivelled round and faced them, a little defiantly.

Joanna said: 'As a matter of fact it looks rather nice. I can't think why, because it really looked rather awful off.'

'But it looks all right on?'

'Yes, quite.'

Mrs Winthorpe turned back to the mirror. She tilted the hat a shade further down over her eyes, raising her chin and slightly turning down the corners of her mouth. She frowned, and blinked two or three times rapidly.

'You're sure now?'

'Yes.'

'It looks – important enough?'

'Yes.'

'Tony?' Mrs Winthorpe turned her head sideways to look at him in the mirror, scrutinising his expression closely for the least hint of amusement.

'You look beautiful, Grandmama!'

So complimentary! And so nice of him to be interested – Alfred never had been. Joanna was very lucky. Tony was a gentleman, whatever Alfred may have said. And he wouldn't do horrible things. . . .

Mrs Winthorpe turned her still suspicious glance back to Joanna. Was there a smile in Joanna's eyes? No, she thought not.

'You really would say if you thought it looked – queer – wouldn't you?'

Her uplifted hands were fluttering, hovering, waiting to remove the hat the moment she was absolutely certain it had passed the test.

'Yes, of course.'

Mrs Winthorpe removed the hat.

'Then I shall wear it,' she pronounced. What a good thing she hadn't sent it to the jumble – or to Cousin Laura!

Joanna started to edge towards the door.

'Are you going now?' said Mrs Winthorpe, and without waiting for an answer she went on: 'I shall just put my feet up for half an hour before we go to the church. Oh, dear . . .' She started to sigh, then she caught the sigh, held it, let it go gently. Almost over now.

But she could not help herself saying: 'I don't want to be cremated after all. It takes far too long.'

IX

Tony closed the door of their bedroom. Then he turned and faced Joanna.

He watched her closely as he said: 'I think you ought to know that your uncles have decided to alter the conditions governing your share of your grandfather's money so that if you ever leave me you should be made to forfeit your income.'

Joanna turned away from his probing eyes. She tried to select, from the confusion in her mind, words to fit into speech.

She stood, with her back to Tony, trying to straighten out her thoughts.

Slowly she realised that she was not afraid. Nor was she particularly worried at the thought of losing her income. She could earn her living if necessary – but it wouldn't be necessary because she would be going to Andrew. She did not even feel hurt. Uncle Harry and Uncle Brian would never do anything to harm her: they were only doing what they thought best, and what hope had they, honest men, kind men, against a confidence trickster like Tony who could deceive the very devil himself if he wanted to!

For a long time she said nothing.

Then 'Have they?' she said. 'Well, I'll tell you now: when I first read the will I thought: I am free! Because I thought I was financially independent. But – the money isn't really important. The important thing is that I'm not going on living with a sham any more. I finally made my mind up last night when I went out on the terrace, while you were asleep – although you said you'd never slept a wink.'

Tony made a movement towards her. 'Don't talk like that, sweet,' he said. 'It's so unkind. I couldn't sleep. I hardly slept at all – I may have just dozed off once or twice – I was so worried about – us.'

'Us? About yourself, you mean. When have you ever cared about anyone but yourself?'

'I had a hard life, sweet – you don't know all of it – I was a very unhappy child.'

'I should think your parents must be a great deal unhappier – No. I'm sorry. That was a cheap gibe.' She rubbed her hand over her forehead. 'Look, Tony, it just won't work any more. I've had enough. Do you understand? I've had enough!'

Yes. He was beginning to understand. He hadn't broken her after all. She really was going to escape him, after all the work he had put in on her. What had gone wrong? How had his tactics failed? He tried once more, the gentle way.

'I do love you, sweet. If I've been difficult in the past, it's only because I've been worried. Things haven't always been easy for me – if I've been cross sometimes, I'll make it up to you now. Just give me – give us! – another chance!'

This was all wrong. *He* begging *her* for a chance! After the way she had behaved! But wait until he got her back where he wanted her. She'd never get up again. He'd make her pay for this, and pay well.

'I love you, sweet,' he said again, clenching his hands with desperation not of love but of hatred.

'You don't really expect me to believe that, do you? After all, you've spent two years telling me how inefficient and useless I am – in private, of course.'

'Well, if you're going to rake up the past. . . .'

'The past is the future, Tony. It is you as you were, are, and will be. It's the real you, unmasked.'

'It was only because I . . .'

'Oh, I know *why* it was! You wanted to break me down, get me completely unsure of myself and under your thumb – after all, you caught me young, didn't you? – get the way all clear for when Grandfather died and I came into money!'

'Joanna!' He took a step towards her.

'And do you know,' she went on, without giving him a chance to say any more, 'you nearly succeeded! Congratulate yourself on that! You really had me convinced that I was lazy, stupid, inefficient, careless – and I tried like hell to do better, to live up to you. To you! What a laugh!'

She watched the blood suffuse his face. How much more was he going to take without losing his temper? She went on:

'Andrew made me think again, and think that perhaps I wasn't as bad as you made out. But I still hadn't the strength to get away – even Andrew couldn't get me out of that net. I had to get out of it myself – and you helped me. You over-played your hand.'

She saw his eyes narrow almost imperceptibly and she thought: he's going to remember this, carefully, so as not to make the same mistake next time.

'You see,' she said, 'it was all very well to keep on telling me that I was inefficient, that might work – did work in fact – but when it comes to telling me that *you* are catching *my* inefficiency, then to anyone with the slightest sense of humour, the whole thing becomes a farce. If it hadn't been for you and your hot-water tap, I might still have been afraid of you – but you can't be afraid of something ridiculous, can you, now can you? – and I might never have realised that something so perfect on top could be so rotten underneath.'

He jerked his head back almost as though she really had spat in his face.

'It's you that are rotten.' His voice was no longer soft, and there was an unfamiliar twang in it. 'You're a whore.'

'No, I'm not,' she said steadily. 'Although you did your best to turn me into one this morning. If you did something for me, I should do something for you – remember?'

He took another step towards her, and she looked up into his red face and staring eyes without flinching.

'Even your uncles are against you. They think you've behaved rottenly.'

'My foolish uncles? That's how you think of them, isn't it? We're all fools to you, aren't we? Oh, I've been watching you this last day or two: "You have a very beautiful granddaughter" and "How's business, Brian?" and "Can I help you, Harry?" – and I know what you've been thinking all the time. My uncles – they were fair game for you. They do their best for everyone, and believe the best of everyone. Well, so far they've only had your version of this marriage. Now they're going to hear mine.'

'They'll never believe you.'

'They'll find it hard to believe. You've acted your part very well.' Tony looked away from her furious eyes. 'All the same, I think they will believe me. My mother was their sister, and they were very fond of her. They're fond of me, too, you know, just as I am of them, in spite of your efforts to turn them all against me so that I would be more than ever in your power.' She watched that barb sink home. 'Even if they do go ahead with their plan, it's not going to make the slightest difference. I'm not going to spend another fifty years with a man I neither love nor respect and end up like Granny, tired and beaten – I wouldn't do that for all the money in the world!'

'I won't set you free. I'll never divorce you.'

'Then maybe I'll divorce you! Besides, you know, the fun of making me suffer will soon begin to pall. It won't be profitable enough. You'll want to be free to look around for another heiress, so I should get rid of me as quickly as you can. And next time, make sure the grandfather – or father – approves of you, because it would make things a lot easier for you to get your hands on money that isn't left in trust. Handling income for her isn't going to be nearly as much fun as handling her capital!'

Tony turned his back on her and walked over to the window. She felt suddenly out of breath, as though she had been running very fast.

He swung round on her. 'You don't imagine Andrew will still be waiting for you, do you? You haven't spoken to him for over two months. Or so you said.'

'That's true. Or, at least, it was true until this morning. Then, when I was sure, quite, quite sure about you, I telephoned him. I am seeing him tomorrow. I shan't be coming back with you tonight, Tony – or ever again. I'm going to talk to my family – all of them – after you've gone.'

He made a final effort. 'You can't do this to us.'

God! she thought. Theatrical to the last.

'I'm sorry, Tony, but I've done it.'

He sat down on the bed and buried his face in his hands in an attitude of despair until he heard the door close behind her. Then he stood up, pulled his suitcase from under the bed and began to pack his things into it. He would put it in the back of the car ready to leave immediately after the service in the churchyard. There was no point in staying any longer.

As he went over to the washbasin to get his shaving kit, he caught sight of Joanna's diamond engagement ring lying on the glass shelf. He picked it up and twisted it round and round in his fingers. That had cost him a couple of hundred – it would be worth more now. It was a good diamond, and good diamonds always appreciated. She'd no right to wear it now! Why the hell should she? He slipped it into his pocket, and went on with his packing.

X

At the gate of the churchyard, the family fell easily into correct order.

Mrs Winthorpe, on Jack's arm, led the way through the graveyard, followed by Elizabeth, Laurine, Joanna. Harry and Brian walked side by side. Tony followed, a little distance behind.

They wound their way among the graves to where Mr Russell stood beside a small, neat hole in the family plot.

There they gathered.

Jack held the ends of the sling on which he was to lower the casket. He waited for a signal from Mr Russell.

'O, merciful God, the Father of our Lord Jesus Christ, who is the resurrection and the life, in whom whosoever believeth shall live, though he die; and whosoever liveth and believeth in him shall not die eternally.'

More promises of eternal life, thought Mrs Winthorpe wearily. But she didn't *want* eternal life. She just wanted to be allowed to rest. She was so tired.

Jack looked askance at Mr Russell, but found no direction in the calm gaze. He let the sling remain limp between his fingers.

He felt Laurine's eyes upon him and suddenly felt benevolent, all powerful, a giver of life, a father of men. He drew himself up, threw his chest out a little. . . .

Then in response to Mr Russell's nod and the slight gesture of his hand towards the grave, he stepped up to the edge of the hole, tautening the sling as he did so.

He lifted the casket, balanced carefully, over the lip of the earth, allowed it to hang poised for a few seconds; then he lowered his arm and the casket swung slowly down out of sight.

Harry peered down the hole to look at the casket. Did it rest straight? Was all in order?

'Earth to earth, ashes to ashes, dust to dust, in sure and certain hope of the resurrection to eternal life. . . .'

Oh, no! prayed Mrs Winthorpe. Peace, peace. . . .

Brian's eyes stung with sudden tears. The Old Man was really gone now. He turned to Elizabeth and felt her sympathy touch him like a kind hand.

'The grace of our Lord Jesus Christ, and the love of God, and the fellowship of the Holy Ghost, be with us all evermore.'

Each of them turned for a final backward glance at the grave.

Then they filtered slowly through the churchyard towards the gate.

As Joanna passed through the gate she started to walk more quickly. Death was behind her. Life lay ahead.

Soon, now, she would be with Andrew. Soon!

She is still young, thought Mrs Winthorpe, with a sudden sharp pang of envy, as she watched Joanna walk along the lane.

Oh, to be young and full of hope. The old life lay behind her in the churchyard . . . Alfred lay there. The new life lay ahead.

But the new life would be no different from the old. For her, there never would be any difference now.

For her, it was too late.

Persephone Books publishes the following titles: